NORMAN TUTTLE

ON THE

LAST FRONTIER

NORMAN TUTTLE

ON THE

LAST FRONTIER

A NOVEL IN STORIES

TOM BODETT

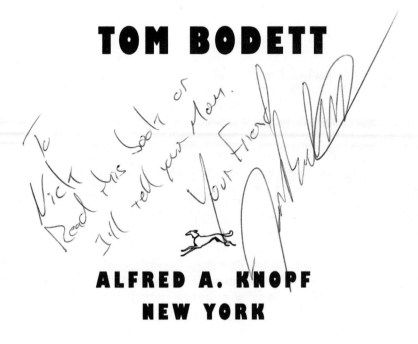

To Nick
Read this book or
I'll tell your Mom.
Your Friend

ALFRED A. KNOPF
NEW YORK

To Rita,
who makes loving easy

THIS IS A BORZOI BOOK PUBLISHED BY ALFRED A. KNOPF

Text copyright © 2004 by Tom Bodett
Jacket illustration copyright © 2004 by Dennis Ziemienski

www.randomhouse.com/teens

Library of Congress Cataloging-in-Publication Data
Bodett, Tom.
Norman Tuttle on the last frontier : a novel in stories / by Tom Bodett.
p. cm.
SUMMARY: Episodes in the life of Alaskan teenager Norman Tuttle, as he grows from
ages thirteen to fifteen, falls in love for the first time, and deepens his relationship
with his father.
ISBN 0-679-89031-9 (trade) — ISBN 0-679-99031-3 (lib. bdg.)
[1. Fathers and sons—Fiction. 2. Love—Fiction. 3. Interpersonal relations—Fiction.
4. Family life—Alaska—Fiction.] I. Title.
PZ7.B63363No 2004
[Fic]—dc22
2003069486

Printed in the United States of America
November 2004
10 9 8 7 6 5 4 3 2 1
First Edition

CONTENTS

ACKNOWLEDGMENTS

Many thanks to Jeff Dwyer, who found Norman Tuttle hiding in some adult books of mine in 1995. He was nuts enough to call me out of the clear blue sky and suggest I might try writing these stories again for young readers. I told him I didn't think so, but was myself nuts enough to become his friend.

Don't ever make friends with an Irishman if you want to continue to have your way. If it wasn't for Jeff and his steadfast sidekick, Elizabeth O'Grady, I would have done something else. And I would have ended up one book and two very good friends short of a rich, full life. Sometimes it's best to just let the Irish have their way with you.

I don't know if Nancy Hinkel is Irish, but she's a mighty fine editor, and I'm grateful for her wise and solid guidance throughout the making of this book, as well as that of Joan Slattery—another fine Irish hand and great editor. It is an honor to work with them both.

Thanks, as ever, to Luana Stovel and Jim Roe for making our business and our friendship possible over hill and dale and ocean. Trust and love and some awfully good work keep us going.

And most of all—thanks to my wife, Rita, and my sons, Courtney and Ben. You make it all happen for me. There's nothing more to say.

TO BEGIN WITH

Norman Tuttle grew up in a place called Alaska. You've probably heard of it—the Last Frontier, all that stuff. I bet you've never heard of Norman Tuttle. He was just a kid there. Kids in Alaska don't know they're growing up on the Last Frontier. It's just what they see on the license plates, and it's something tourists like to say a lot because they've never been around so many mountains and moose before.

It's not like Alaska isn't wilderness—it mostly is. But most Alaskans don't live in the wild. They live on the edge of the wild in towns with schools and cable TV and stores and dentists and roller rinks sometimes. It's just like anyplace else, only with mountains and moose. At least that's what it feels like if you grow up there like Norman Tuttle did.

Norman's dad was a fisherman and the family owned their own boat, the *Francine,* named after Norman's mom. The boat was wooden and usually smelled bad. Fishing boats smell that way no matter who you name them after. Fishing was a busy job. Uncle Stu and Norman's dad were gone a lot of the time from May to September chasing after salmon. Then in the fall they would change the gear on the boat from nets to longlines and they'd fish for halibut, then cod, until deep into the winter. The boat always needed something: props, rudders, engines, radar, paint and putty. It kept his dad and Uncle Stu pretty busy even when they weren't gone fishing. It seemed to Norman that his dad had a lot more time for fishing than he had for anything else.

Norman's mom did everything moms do, only probably more of it, like most women who marry fishermen. Norman helped with the housework and keeping track of the littler kids, and if anybody asked her about him, she would have to say he was a good kid.

Fishing was a pretty decent way to make a living and Norman had everything he needed and a few things he didn't, including his little brothers, Franky and Caleb, and middle sister, Jessie. Their house was a normal, square, straight-up-and-down house-type house on a dirt road on the edge of town. Norman had his own bedroom, which looked toward the bay and the mountains across it and was probably one of the most beautiful views on the planet Earth. If you were into views.

Norman's best friend, Stanley, lived just down the road. They'd spend most of their time together ranging through the fields of fireweed playing war, or jigging for flounder down in the boat harbor, or riding their bikes to the Saturday movies. It was a normal childhood for a place like that, and it's hard to say exactly when it ended.

It's like driving to Alaska from someplace else. You get to Canada first, which looks about like where you just were, only now it's called Canada. Then after a while it starts to look like something else again. There are fewer buildings, more mountains, and blue glaciers. Tundra bogs and wildflowers and big, goofy-looking moose appear alongside the road, and then pretty soon a sign comes up that says Welcome to Alaska, the Last Frontier. Where does one thing end and the next one start? Wherever they say it does.

It's the same thing with growing up. One day you're a kid going along like you always do with everything looking the same as it's been, and then something happens to you. This is what happened on the Last Frontier to a kid named Norman Tuttle.

LOST AND FOUND

Not many things come easy when you're thirteen, but Norman didn't have much trouble falling off his dad's fishing boat. Actually, he was pretty much designed to succeed at just such a thing. Having grown over six inches since Christmas, he found that his arms and legs stretched into territory he was not entirely familiar with. In short, Norman was a klutz. He would grow out of it, his mother had assured him, but probably not before he came face to foam with the black icy waters of southeast Alaska.

Norman had come out on deck to "answer nature's call," as some say. But he didn't just answer it. He leaped at it. He'd propped his legs against the low boat rail in the dark with his overlong shins, and his feet had simply gone out from under him. His brief few moments in midair were spent desperately trying to put himself away rather than concentrating on a graceful entry. If you've ever felt the chill of Alaska waters, you will understand his preoccupation on the way in, and let's face it, there is no pretty way to fall off a fishing boat.

Landing face first, mouth open, is also no way to prepare for the next step—hollering for help. During what seemed like the eternity it took for Norman to clear the salt water from his throat enough to scream for help, he watched as the boat chugged steadily away in the darkness.

"*Daaaad!*"

"*Daaaaaaad!!*"

"*Uncle Stu!*"

The throb of the propeller still pulsed against his body.

"*Daaad! Wait! Daaad,* Dad, oh no, oh God."

Norman tried swimming after the boat, but he stopped once to slip out of his deck shoes, and when he looked back up he'd lost sight of the single white stern light. He could still hear the prop in the water, but it had no direction. Nothing had direction. The overcast sky was black. The water was black. The shoreline they'd been following couldn't be far off, but it could be anywhere he pointed.

There is probably no good time to be in a situation like this, but being in this situation at age thirteen has got to be the worst of them. You're too old to cry and too young to swear, and you don't even have much of a life to go flashing past. Norman was stunned, but only temporarily. There's a call for action built into people of any age that comes into play at these times. It's called panic, and Norman proceeded to do exactly that.

Clawing at the water like a drowning man—and not being too far off the mark—Norman thrashed his way toward what he figured to be the direction of shore. Panic not lending itself to clear thinking, it never occurred to Norman he might be swimming out to sea. Which was just as well, because he wasn't.

As he made his way along, the adrenaline subsided and his strokes became long and even. He knew he was moving at a good pace now. As he started to think again, the first thing he thought was, This is freaking cold. He was already losing feeling in his legs, and his throat was getting a knot in it like he'd just eaten ice cream too fast. I'm going to freeze to death and die, he thought. Then he laughed, and in the process gulped a mouthful of water. You dummy, of course if you freeze to death you die, and he laughed again. The cold was taking its toll on Norman's mental processes, and just as he was about to let it all sink into a giggling fit that would have certainly killed him, he heard it—*bonk!* Then he felt it.

"Ow!" he cried, grabbing his forehead.

Although Norman realized that only *he* could actually find a place to bump his head in the wide ocean, it was the most welcome goose egg he'd ever awarded himself, or ever be likely to. Reaching his arms out in front of him, he felt the scaly surface of a barnacle-covered piling.

It was standing straight up and down in the water, and after wrapping himself around it in a grateful embrace he realized that it wasn't floating. The piling was attached to the earth, Norman was attached to the piling, and for a minute or two life was good again. He panted with relief at the notion he'd swum in the right direction.

Norman's thinking was getting pretty sticky by this point, so it took a while for it to sink in that he was still going to freeze to death and die, even if he was in the company of several hundred well-grounded barnacles. Venturing a look up the piling to see what it might be attached to, he saw that it was, in fact, attached to thin air. Only inches above his head it stopped short of any hope of holding up a building, and far short of salvation.

Still, thin air was better than cold water. Reaching up, he felt the flat top of the piling and, using everything he had left, managed to haul his wet hide onto it. While draped over the top belly down, Norman's squeezed bladder reminded him he had not finished the business he'd gone out on deck for in the first place. It felt warm—secretly wonderful—and tears came at the thought of it.

The damp late summer air also felt warm compared to the water, and although Norman was shivering uncontrollably, he managed to sit up straight on the piling and let the feeling come back to his legs.

If it had been light enough for anyone to see him, Norman would have been a sorry sight—a quivering creature swaddled in wet wool and mounted on a stick like some toy ready to be brought to life. If you pulled a string at the bottom, he might rise up and wave, or dispense a candy.

But Norman didn't rise up and wave. He just sat, shook, and worried. He knew that his dad and Uncle Stu hadn't seen him go out on deck. They were in the pilothouse drinking coffee and complaining about fish like they always did at the end of a trip. Fish too few. Price too low. Fish and Game regulations too stupid for words. But they found words— hours of them.

Norman would usually ignore their grousing and kick a nest into the pile of dirty clothes and blankets on his bunk to curl up in and read magazines, as he always did at the end of a trip. He'd read these issues a dozen times each. It was a real dork-o-rama of outdated copies of *National Geographic* and *Reader's Digest*—everything that piled up on the back of the toilet at home and was eventually shoveled onto the boat. Every once in a while *National Geo* would have a cool picture of a tribe from tropical New Guinea, or a short skirt in a street scene in Madrid might cause a page to become marked, but mostly the magazines were an exercise in page flipping, something to pass the time until he fell asleep or somebody came back to graciously tell him they were pulling into port. "Get your gear on, Norman. Time to unload."

Unless one of the men decided to go back and look in on him, they wouldn't know he was gone until they got to town, which was still hours away. They wouldn't look in on him. Norman knew that for sure.

Norman was mostly tolerated and largely ignored on the boat. His dad and Uncle Stu had fished together since they were kids. They always did the same things, they always said the same things, and a bashful boy who couldn't walk a straight line on land or sea did not fit easily into their routine. It was his mother's idea to send him along on these few late-summer halibut trips.

"It will be good for Norman," she said apologetically to his dad, who was on his hands and knees mopping up the spilled can of engine oil Norman had kicked over onto the dock while putting his gear aboard for that first exciting trip.

"It will be good for Norman. It will be good for Norman, but what is Norman good for?" his dad had snapped back to her. Norman was not supposed to hear that, so it's exactly what stuck in his head and took the fun out of that first trip and every one after it.

It was still stuck in his head as he sat on his piling in the dark. What is Norman good for? What is Norman good for? Cold and chattering, he wrapped his arms as far around himself as he could and tried to think of two things he was good for.

He was good for chopping bait. But then he was always cutting holes in his gloves, and that made his dad mad. "Those things cost money, ya know," he'd say, and toss

Norman a fresh pair, which Norman always managed to fumble and drop.

He was good for coiling line, then. That's about the only other thing they ever let him do. But a lot of the lines he coiled went off the deck in a big tangled wad when they tried to make a set.

"When you going to learn to turn a coil, Norman?" his dad would say. "Stand aside and let your uncle do that. Fixing your messes takes time. Time is money, young man."

Norman settled on the fact that maybe he was only good for costing money. And here he was doing it again. He'd fallen off the boat, and his dad would have to turn around to come find him. It never occurred to Norman that his dad would be anything but angry about this. He pictured the boat swinging up to the piling to rescue him, his dad on deck—red-faced, shaking his head. He'd yank him on board without a word, then mumble on his way back to the pilot-house, "Try to stay with us this time, all right?"

Norman suddenly hated his father.

"Try to stay with *this*, old man." Norman flung out a fist and his balance changed. In a gut-clenching instant he looked down and saw that the tide was falling fast. His stocking feet were a good four feet from the water, though just a while ago they'd been nearly touching it. The sensation almost made him fall over, and he became panicky with the realization that the tide had probably another twenty feet to go before it ebbed. The top of his piling would be as high as a two-story house in a matter of hours.

Norman was terrified of high places. He'd discovered this only a month ago when his dad had sent him up the mast to replace a fitting. He'd gotten only halfway before he had to stop. He'd clung to the rigging like a little bear and cried until Uncle Stu climbed up to get him. His dad had never said a word, just stood there with that red face, shaking his head.

That's how he'll find me, Norman thought. Trembling and crying and holding on to this piling. Norman wanted to fall in the water and simply float away. But the thought of it made him even colder. His shivering had become convulsive, and it was likely he would knock himself back in the water.

"I've *got* to stop shaking," he said out loud, and he heard something that sounded like his dad in his voice. It suddenly seemed unavoidable.

"I'm *going* to stop shaking," he said louder. He liked the sound of it, and tried different ways of putting it. "I'm going to *stop* shaking." "*I'm* going to stop *shaking!*" "*I'm gonna stop shaking!*" he yelled into the night, and sat motionless as the ring of it evaporated from his ears.

When all was quiet again, he became aware of himself.

His hands were on his hips. He was sitting tall and firm. And he wasn't shaking. The piling swayed under him like a calm, determined horse.

"Well, would you look at that," he remarked, now enjoying the company of his own voice. "It worked." He grinned and yanked up his drooping socks one at a time while he thought of more.

"Okay, everybody, listen up!" Norman assumed an admiral's posture, one arm crooked behind his back, and swung his head from side to side so that all of the quiet night could hear it.

"I'm gonna sit on top of this pole, I'm not gonna shake, I'm not going to fall in the water, I'm not going to cry, and I'm not going to do all those things all night long if I have to." He snapped his head forward and suddenly there were other things to say.

"And when my dad gets here I'm going to sit on this pole like it's never been sat on. It's going to be, 'Look at Norman sit on that pole now, will you, Stu?' "

Norman posed. "Yeah. Look at me, Stu. Look at me, old man. This is Norman speaking. Norman Tuttle. He can fall off a boat in Alaska in the middle of the night and live to tell about it. No thanks to you."

He paused for a long time. He'd never heard his voice used with such conviction before. It lent an importance to what he was saying, and Norman felt compelled to say important things.

"I've been doing some thinking up here on this pole, ol' man." Norman stroked his chin dramatically. "An' I been thinking none of this would've happened if you'd paid a little more attention to what was going on around here. None of this would've happened if you'd paid a little more attention to your deckhand!" He let his words ring in the air, then spoke more quietly to the truth of the thing. "None of this would have happened if you'd paid more attention to your son."

The tears came again, and he couldn't stop them. They leaked from his clenched eyes, and he wiped them clear with his clenched fists. He threw six, seven, eight punches at the empty night and almost fell off the piling in the process.

He saw the water was now better than twelve feet below him. It made him dizzy and Norman groped the empty air for something to hold on to. Finding nothing, he swayed with the rocking piling and clamped his legs with his hands as if to keep them there. "I'm not. Going to fall. In the water," he said deliberately. "You left me here. And I'm going to sit. Right here."

And sit he did. He might have sat there all night. He might have sat there all the next day too if he had to, but he didn't. No sooner had he assembled and locked himself into his permanent sitting position—hands on knees, head straight, eyes forward—than a searchlight appeared around a point hidden in the darkness. It was his dad and Uncle Stu. He could hear them.

"Nooorrman."

That's Uncle Stu, thought Norman.

"Normy!"

That's Dad.

Norman didn't feel like hollering anything just yet. Let them look a minute or two more, he thought. Then it registered—*Normy?* His dad hadn't called him that in forever. Not since he was a little kid wrestling on the living room rug. Not since he'd learned how to ride a bike. *Normy.* Norman's string was pulled.

"Here, Dad, I'm over here!" Norman rose up and waved his arms in the air. The searchlight found the piling, worked its way upward, and met his eyes with a welcome stab of pain. He heard the engine growl and saw the boat swing toward him. His dad was on the bow holding the light.

"Normy, are you all right?" His dad's voice sounded odd. Was he mad? No, Norman knew too well what mad sounded like. It was something else. Something urgent. The sound of it washed over Norman like a warm wind.

"Good to go," Norman said, meaning it. "No problems." He could hear his dad talking to Uncle Stu at the wheel.

"Easy, easy now. Don't hit the piling. Easy, Stu, darn it! You'll knock him off there. Normy, can you climb down?"

"You bet." It seemed that Normy could, in fact, do things that Norman couldn't. Forgetting his fear of high places, he shinnied down the piling and stepped gingerly onto the deck. His knees started to buckle, but he stopped them and instead let them quake for a second or two. Then he straightened up to look his dad in the face for the first time.

When Norman saw the tears come to his father's eyes, he had to look away. When he felt the big arms come around him, he stiffened, but the arms stayed.

"Oh, Normy, Normy," his father was saying in his ear. "I thought I'd lost you."

Norman just stood there with a lump in his throat the size of a deck winch. He took his father's warmth and sound and smell and wrapped them around himself like the blanket Uncle Stu was pulling over his shoulders.

His dad gave one last big squeeze and stepped back, wiping at his own tears—curious about them, and surprised.

Norman took one step back, tripped over the hatch cover, and fell into the hold full of fish. His dad and Uncle Stu lunged to catch him but got only the blanket. As Norman lay on his back looking up at their alarmed faces, he felt a flush of blood coming to his cheeks, as it did every time he let his father down. His dad's look of fear melted away, and his head began to move back and forth. That familiar head shaking. Familiar, but changed. In place of the scowl was a smile. A smile as wide and warm and full of promise as that hold was full of fish.

THANKSGIVING CHEER

It was a good Thanksgiving that year. The best. It became one of those momentous occasions for Norman that, even at the age of thirteen, he knew would stay with him for as long as he lived.

The day started out quietly enough. Norman and his dad worked together in the basement most of the morning putting away fishing gear and cleaning up to make room for the houseful of relatives due to invade that afternoon. Norman's mother was in the kitchen cooking and running herd on the Three Creepies—the two younger brothers and a sister who were going nuts with excitement about the occasion. Even though they had no idea what the occasion was.

Norman knew what it was and he didn't care. He was enjoying the time with his dad in the basement. Ever since the accident on the fishing boat three months before, there was something new going on between them. Norman wasn't quite sure what it was about, but his dad was.

While the father had searched aimlessly for the son in the dark, he'd had a few hours to look at what kind of father he was. The kind who thought it was a father's job to whip a son into shape and tell him where he messed up. The kind who thought hard love saved the world from soft children. Most painful of all, Norman's dad realized he was the kind of father who could be chattering about nonsense in the pilothouse of a boat and not even notice his boy fall overboard and disappear without a trace.

During the search the elder Tuttle had made a pact with his god. He swore that if he got his boy back, he would never treat him like he was in the way again. Even when he was. He wouldn't make him feel stupid. Even when he did dumb things. He would stop expecting him to be more than the poor clumsy kid he was right now. And he would love him. Not just tell him he loved him, but live that way. Standing on the deck that dark night holding his soggy son in his arms, he knew it was a vow he would keep.

And he was keeping it. He'd taken him duck hunting for the first time, and Norman, to the delight of both of them, did not blow his or anybody else's foot off. "Nice shooting, Norm. Point that thing over there—not at the dog—yeah, there. Good job."

If he was going down to the gear store for something, he'd remember to ask Norman to tag along. "Wanna see how to go broke fishing?"

He taught him how to play cribbage, and they played a lot.

Well into the damp, dark nights of November, the Tuttle men could be found at the kitchen table counting, "Fifteen-two, fifteen-four, run for three is seven and a pair for nine."

"You missed your nobs. Pay attention."

"I'm winning. *You* pay attention."

"Don't talk to your father in that tone."

"You're jealous."

"You're grounded."

"You're joking." And so it went. They were becoming something like friends.

And as these new friends were cleaning up the basement that Thanksgiving morning, Norman listened while his dad told old army stories. Norman liked these kinds the best because they were always a little spicy and illegal.

His dad stopped sweeping and dropped his voice. "Don't you ever tell your mother about this, but one time when I was stationed at Fort Lewis, me and a few of the boys got into some moonshine, and as you know I don't drink, and I didn't then either, but there were these three dancers, see, and . . ." Off he went on some story that only half made sense to Norman, but it didn't matter because his dad seemed to enjoy the telling, and that was enough for them both.

Norman's day took a decided turn for the worse once they finished in the basement.

"Well," his dad said with an arm over his shoulder, "that oughta give you kids plenty of room to play. Better go get cleaned up, bub. Company's comin' soon." His dad walked past the workbench on his way to the stairs, stopping to put a loose screwdriver back in its holder. "And you kids stay out of my tools." Frank Tuttle climbed out of the basement un-aware he'd just left his son in a smoldering heap of ash.

Kids, Norman thought. It's always *you kids*. I'm thirteen going on fourteen. The Creepies are kids—just a pack of bed-wetting, nose-picking, jelly-faced carpet monkeys. They color on walls. Put beans up their nostrils. They cry about nothing and get "owwies." Those are kids. I'm no kid. I'm a . . . well, I'm, uh . . . I'm . . . not.

Norman slumped onto the bottom step and stared across the freshly swept concrete floor, which suddenly looked as flat and gray as his mood.

Thanksgiving in the Tuttle household was an overrated and predictable affair to Norman. It had been the same thing year after year for as long as he could remember.

Grandma and Grandpa Beal always came, which was no big deal because they lived in town and they saw them al-most every day anyway. They were nice enough but, like most old people, kind of dopey. Grandpa wore a faded blue coverall every day, although he hadn't worked in fifteen years. His thick marine mechanic's hands seemed permanently frozen around an invisible tool. Grandma lived in her apron and all Norman ever saw her do was cook. She smelled vaguely of cookies and pot roast, no matter where she was. Grandma and Grandpa never knew what to do with kids except pat their heads and give them cookies.

The only difference in all of that at Thanksgiving was that Grandma wore her Thanksgiving dress and Grandpa wore a black jacket and tie. Same dress, same jacket and tie. Every year.

"What a pretty dress, Mom," Norman's mom would always say at the door, and "Pop, don't *you* look dashing today." Same every year.

And Grandpa would have a bottle of wine in his hand. Thanksgiving was the only time Norman ever saw alcohol of any kind in the house. It was for the big-deal Thanksgiving toast his dad made every year.

Then Uncle Stu and Aunt Sissy would show up. Norman saw Uncle Stu almost every day, but he didn't see Aunt Sissy much. She was one of those nervous sorts who moved like a chicken. A confused chicken. Always going two steps forward and one back and pivoting her head around looking for who knows what to get into next. Aunt Sissy was a pain in the pants, and she had to know it because except for holidays she hardly ever came around.

All Aunt Sissy did was talk without ever managing to say anything. "Like spit on a skillet," Uncle Stu said once. "Lots of activity, but not much getting accomplished."

The first thing out of her mouth whenever she saw Norman was "My, look at you. How you've grown into such a little man."

Norman had been growing into Aunt Sissy's little man for eight years that he could remember and possibly longer, because now she was saying the same thing to Norman's youngest brother, Caleb, who was only two.

He once overheard his dad say that Aunt Sissy put real horsepower into the term *motor mouth*. She'd go on and on about whatever came to mind without taking a breath, and it didn't seem to matter if anybody paid any attention to her or not. She just liked to listen to herself. A lot more than anybody else did.

And every year, right after Aunt Sissy and Uncle Stu and Grandma and Grandpa, came his mom's sister, Aunt Edna, along with Uncle Elmer. They were okay as far as relatives went, Norman thought. They were nice—and quiet—and Norman's family didn't see them much because they lived up in Anchorage. From the time Norman could walk, Uncle Elmer had shaken his hand. Norman liked that. Uncle Elmer would then pretend to see something in the boy's ear and pull out a fifty-cent piece he had palmed out of sight. Norman used to like that.

Aunt Edna would always remember something he'd done that deserved a compliment: a good grade at school, a bike-rodeo trophy, whatever it was his mom had thought to mention in a letter or phone call. Norman would usually blush and beam and pick at his pant leg.

These people were perfectly okay with Norman except for one thing. Five things, actually. What he dreaded about the arrival of Elmer and Edna were the five cousins they brought with them. The whole chemistry of the house changed when those kids poured in the door.

Norman's mother would mutate into an army staff sergeant and start barking orders. "Shoes off, everybody. Norman, put the coats in the bedroom. Has everyone said hello to Grandma and Grandpa? Norman, I said put away the coats." Everyone would be in the kitchen for a while saying hello while babies crawled around people's feet, toddlers cried, and they all talked at once over Aunt Sissy, who'd be bobbing and weaving across the kitchen.

The adults would allow this ugly business to continue for an excruciating stretch of time, and then Norman's mom would finally issue the order that he'd come to despise.

"Okay, kids, we need room in here. Everybody down to the basement to play until dinner."

And that would be it. They'd all go downstairs and pull out dumb games to play or invent dumber ones or watch television and generally be kids. There would be no more contact with the grown-ups for the rest of the day.

When dinner was ready, the youngsters would be banished to the card tables in the other room so that the adults could enjoy their meal. They would be told to shush when it came time for the toast, a long, drawn-out deal thanking the dear Lord for one thing or the other—good fishing, good health, good food, or some stupid stuff. When they were done, Norman and the rest of the kids would be sent either outside to play or back into the basement.

The adults would wander to the living room to talk in low tones about important things that Norman could only wonder about. This year Norman wasn't sure he belonged in the living room yet, but he knew he didn't belong in the basement anymore.

Like his brothers and sisters, all his cousins were younger than he. It used to be okay, but somewhere along the line hide-and-seek, cooties, and crazy eights had lost their luster for Norman. He was a commercial fisherman, sort of, and he beat his dad at cribbage. That should be worth something to somebody. But, as ever, there are a lot of should-be's in life and too few somethings and somebodies.

The extended Tuttle-Beal clan arrived on schedule and according to formula. Grandma and Grandpa entered with dress and tie and ceremonial bottle of wine. Uncle Stu came with Aunt Sissy, whose mouth hit the deck running: "My, Norman, you've grown into such a little man." And, of course, the grand finale—Aunt Edna, Uncle Elmer, and tribe arrived at peak intensity.

Elmer shook Norman's hand and bent forward to look in his ear. When he produced the fifty cents, though, Norman couldn't even bring himself to smile over it. It was a stupid trick and fifty cents didn't mean what it used to.

Edna leaned down and kissed his forehead and lingered there a second longer, saying quietly, "You were very brave on that piling, Normy. I'm glad you hung on for us."

Norman blushed and picked at his pants. The noise level in the kitchen rose to familiar and dangerous proportions. Voices tried to outmatch each other. Kids shouted to pee or pleaded for juice. One little house possum already had his hands on the cold turkey only to have them slapped away by a babbling aunt. This set up what Norman called the cycle of despair, where hot tempers and high-pitched demands passed through the little kids like a bad case of measles. Bawling babies bumped heads and crawled between legs. Toddlers found places to pinch their fingers. Others complained about theft and insult.

"Maa-aahm! Caleb took my comic book."

"Jessie called me a pigeon!"

"I said *pilgrim.*"

Norman was ordered to put the coats away while everybody jostled to have their heads patted by the grandparents. Then, just as the din reached a fever pitch, Norman heard the cursed announcement: "Okay, kids, we need some room to breathe in here. Everybody to the basement so we can get dinner ready."

Eight young cousins stampeded down the basement stairs to pursue their silliness in private, while one half-young Tuttle stalled for time by the kitchen table, swiping olives from the relish tray Aunt Sissy was preparing. "Norman, you'll spoil your dinner," she said.

Norman's dad was talking and laughing with Uncle Elmer in the corner. When he heard Aunt Sissy, he glanced absently at Norman and said, "Norman, your mother said kids to the basement. Now go."

A scolded pup, Norman looked at his dad, and his heart fell into his socks. Hadn't the man been telling secret stories in the basement not two hours ago? How could he possibly go back down in that room now and play freeze tag or cooties with a bunch of . . . *kids?*

Before he disappeared down the stairs, tail dragging, Norman stopped and took one short, hurtful look back at his father, who at that very moment looked up from his discussion and saw it. It passed as quickly as it came, and nothing was exchanged, only acknowledged.

Norman slunk down the stairs, made his way through the whirling toddlers, and pretended to busy himself arranging things on the workbench. The other kids had four games going on at once. Franky was pushing Jessie on one roller skate in an attempt to run down little Caleb and two tippy cousins, who giggled continually and shrieked, "Help, Norman, help. Help help help help help."

Norman ignored it and pretended to concentrate on the screwdriver he held in his hand. He made a line of increasingly deeper dents in the plywood bench top, ending with a hard stab that left it standing straight up on its own. Pounded by his own thoughts, he absently tapped at the screwdriver with a ball-peen hammer. Slowly the blade and shaft began disappearing into the wood.

Upstairs, meanwhile, his dad was having some thoughts of his own. As he and Norman's mom primped for dinner in their bedroom, he spoke them. "Francine, I see Norm's put out about something, but I can't figure out what's going on. We had a perfectly fine morning together. I know the kid's sensitive, but I can't believe he'd pout over Sissy busting him for sneaking olives. So I sent him downstairs. It's

Thanksgiving. That's where kids go on Thanksgiving. He say anything to you?"

Francine Tuttle smoothed her dress in front of the closet mirror. "I think he said it all to you, Frank." She turned her back to him. "Zip me."

It wasn't until Frank watched Grandpa Beal pouring the wine into the glasses before dinner that the problem became clear to him. He remembered the year, and it wasn't that long ago, that Francine's father had passed the responsibility for the Thanksgiving toast to him. "Frank," he'd said simply, "this is your house. Would you do us the honor, sir?"

And an honor it had been to stand, lift his glass, and recount the Tuttle blessings as he saw them. The Beal and Tuttle clans were teetotalers, so having the wine at dinner was a lot more glamour than appeal. No one had ever really asked where the tradition started, and no one had ever finished a glass of wine either, but the tradition endured.

Thinking about the toast and still puzzling over his oldest boy, Frank Tuttle made an inspired guess. He quietly set another place at the big table.

When Aunt Sissy called the kids for dinner, Norman was the last body to slink up the stairs. He was looking at his feet as he walked past the big dining table and didn't see his dad until a hand reached out and touched his shoulder.

"Norm," his father said, "why don't you join us?"

There are just a few grand occasions in this life that stay with a person all the way to the end—winning a soccer game with a parent in the stands, surprise parties, laughing so hard with your best friend that food comes out your nose. These giddy moments flutter over a life like tournament flags, and this was certainly one of Norman's. He'd always remember standing for the first time shoulder to shoulder with the grown-ups, a mysterious half glass of dark red wine in his hand, while his father made the toast and prayer.

"Dear Lord," he began, head bowed. Norman glanced into the other room and frowned at his brother Franky, who was holding two green olives up to his eyes, trying to make the little kids crack up. Norman slowly shook his head and then bowed it, listening to his father.

"Thank you for good fishing, and a fair price. We will make it through another winter warm and well fed. And thank you for our health and the continued good health of Grandma and Grandpa Beal. Thank you for another year of peace in our little part of the world. These are dangerous times, and you have once again spared those we love from the grief of war. Thank you for my four healthy and spirited children."

He paused here and looked up, catching Norman looking back at him. "And thank you most especially for bringing my oldest boy back to me to grow into such a fine young man."

Norman clinked his glass with his father's. They both cleared their throats. Glasses were tinging all around. Then the young man sipped at the strange wine, and as the bitterness left his tongue, he wondered how he was going to get that screwdriver out of the workbench top before the end of the day.

POINT OF NO RETURN

It all started in algebra class. Right in the middle of Mrs. Polquist's discussion on the Pythagorean theorem. It was a theorem Norman would never remember, but he would always know the moment he'd noticed girls for the first time.

Of course, Norman had noticed girls before. He knew pretty much what they were and how they were put together. They had just never done anything for him until now. Norman and his best friend, Stanley Bindel, would sometimes look through the magazines Uncle Stu kept hidden in their net shed down at the harbor. Until now they had mostly giggled at the pictures for a while, gotten bored, and gone back to chucking rocks at seagulls.

But now those magazines intrigued and embarrassed Norman. His and Stan's laughter became more forced. Norman found himself thinking about the pictures long after they'd been put away.

It was all brought on in one singular moment by the actions of Laura Magruder, who sat in the next row one seat up. She'd dropped her pencil and it rolled toward

Norman. He pushed it back to her with his foot without even thinking. When she rose again with the pencil in her hand, she looked at Norman with a smile of thanks.

It was an innocent smile—at least it was meant to be. And it was genuine. But it was also a smile that for the first time in Norman's life he recognized as being *sexy*. Norman had been smiled at before without any noticeable side effects, but this one was different.

A flood of emotions from passion to panic filled him up and glowed red in his face.

The midday breaking news: at 2:35 p.m. on January 18, Norman Tuttle—age thirteen—reached puberty.

Norman spent the rest of that class somewhere east of the planet Venus. By the time the bell rang he had studied every hair on Laura Magruder's head and fallen in love with them individually. He had studied the pattern in her knit sweater until it made shapes on his retina wall like some religious hologram. He had memorized the folds in her jeans and the smudges on her white running shoes.

He imagined her feet moving, and where they walked, and if they walked home, and what color her bedroom was, and on through the rest of the hour. When she made a movement, no matter how slight, his heart would seize.

He bit the eraser clean off his pencil when she turned to look at the clock over his head, almost catching him staring.

It was the first time Norman had ever regretted hearing the school bell. It rang like a lousy alarm clock jarring him out of a wonderful dream where everything was in color and he was winning.

As the other kids, including Laura, jumped out of their seats and crowded through the door, Norman lingered at his desk putting his things away carefully, hesitant to step out into a world that had so completely changed since he came to class.

Norman stood in the schoolyard watching the daily chaos unfold around kids loading onto buses, or meeting their moms in cars, or wandering off in twos and threes. He was looking for her. He didn't know why, or what he'd do if he found her, but nothing in all creation seemed more important at the moment.

"Well, if it isn't ol' Stormin' Norman." It was Stanley saying hello and throwing a snowball at the same time.

"Knock it off, Stan," Norman said, brushing the snow out of his hair, genuinely annoyed.

"What did ya do, flunk your algebra quiz?"

Norman looked suspiciously at Stanley for a second, then blurted, "Algebra doesn't have anything to do with it."

"Anything to do with what?"

"Nothing, anything to do with nothing . . ." Norman would have stammered on and probably given up the story, but just then he saw her over Stan's shoulder.

She was walking with two of her friends, talking and laughing. Just as she crossed behind Stan, she looked up from her friends and their eyes met. It was there again. *What* was there again? *It*, that look, those eyes and that smile. The smile that boiled Norman's ears and sent a blast of white heat from his forehead to his big feet.

Laura looked away with a snap of her head and picked up the pace of her trio. The whole thing couldn't have taken more than half a second, but it was long enough to set into motion a complex chain of biological and emotional trip switches in Norman.

Norman's body reacted to the signals and began an intricate series of functions that he didn't fully understand at the moment. With no more self-control than a sleepwalker, he saw himself fix on the object of his affections, release a snowball with deadly accuracy, and hit his target square in the middle of the back.

She turned around angrily. Her friends giggled into their mittens, and then all three ran off.

"What the heck did you do that for?" Stanley said.

"She was asking for it," Norman said back.

The formal courtship of Laura Magruder had begun.

The next couple of weeks were hard on Norman. He spent every day at school ignoring Laura Magruder and every night at home worshiping her. While Norman ignored Laura she continued to ignore and even actively avoid him. So he knew that the relationship was going well. He found himself racing from science to algebra class so he could watch her walk in rather than the other way around. He memorized all her clothes and wondered what she'd wear next.

He hadn't done an algebra assignment in ten days. Mrs. Polquist did not buy his excuse that the Three Creepies continued to sneak into his book bag to destroy them.

He hadn't played cribbage with his dad in a week. "It's just boring," he'd grouse, then return to his room and stare at the ceiling.

Even Stanley Bindel, tired of Norman's silence and absent-mindedness, stopped seeking him out after school. "I don't know what I said or did to you, Norman. Just let me know when you get over it."

For the first time ever, Norman had a secret so personal that he couldn't share it with his best friend. He might have shared it if he'd understood it himself, but he didn't. Not everything.

He didn't know why some of those gushy songs on the radio now made sense. Why he even looked forward to a few of them. Norman had never had any interest in music at all before. Now he found himself huddled with his clock radio during those marathon ceiling-gazing sessions in the bedroom.

And it was the same thing with television. He understood so many more things than he used to. Overnight, like he'd taken a smart pill, stories of unrequited love, terminally ill sweethearts, and lonely soldiers rang clear in Norman's head. He could feel it. Comprehend it. He knew something. What was it he knew? And how could he tell Stanley?

In truth, Norman didn't think too much about Stanley. He didn't think too much about anything except Laura. *Laura.* He'd say the word in his thoughts but couldn't bring himself to speak it. Whom would he say it to? What if somebody heard? Norman took up full-time residence in his own head.

His fantasies kept him awake far into the night. He'd be a battle-bloodied soldier returning from war, his face blackened with combat, his shirt torn, and his shoulders held bravely back despite a bad limp from a festering leg wound. Laura would run in slow motion out to the gate and press into his arms. They'd spin and laugh and look deeply into each other's eyes, and finally they'd kiss.

Or he'd be in a hospital, torn apart in the execution of some courageous deed on Laura's behalf. She would be stroking his hand, making promises as he bore his pain and held her eyes with his. And then they'd kiss.

The later at night, the better the fantasy, and eventually Norman would become a superman—a nearly invulnerable fighting machine who could ward off all attackers with his highly trained hands and feet. And always in the background, quaking with fear and bursting with pride, would be Laura watching Super Norman rip his way through a gang of bikers. Or a communist horde. Or a horde of communist bikers. Always with pluck and venom, and always victorious. Laura would run to her hero at the end of the fray and they would embrace. And then they'd kiss.

Norman always stopped with the kissing part because he didn't really know what came next. When you are the older brother of Three Creepies and the biggest and wisest of all your cousins, you don't get much information on the opposite sex. He had some idea. He wasn't stupid and you couldn't watch TV for twenty minutes, even at the end of the road in Alaska, without getting the drift of what men and women do with each other when nobody is looking. But still, kissing was as far as Norman was willing to flesh out the fantasy at this point.

While refusing to take the next step in his head, there soon came a time for the next step in the real world of Norman Tuttle and Laura Magruder. A serious steady relationship cannot last on the merits of one well-placed snowball. They were going to have to go on a date. This is where Norman really ran into a dark and scary alley. The methods of asking a girl out were infinitely more obscure than what came after a good kiss.

There were few people in Norman's life who had the experience he needed right now. But there was one in particular who just might be able to help him out. As long as he played his cards right.

That evening, after the little kids had gone off to bed and his mom had retired to her sewing room, Norman let his dad talk him into a game of cribbage in the kitchen.

"Well, Normy. Long time no see. What you been up to all week?" His dad dealt the cards.

"Not much."

"Haven't seen Stanley around lately. You guys have a fight or something?"

"No." Norman hunched his shoulders and tried to concentrate on his cards.

The elder Tuttle seemed to know something was going on but hesitated to keep stabbing for it. Norman would come out with it when he was ready.

He was ready.

"Dad, if you had to ask a girl out on a date, how would you do it?" The words were blurted out across the table like a spilled soda.

The father sat silent. Absorbing it. Relaxing into the question. He may have feared worse problems than girls.

"Well, Norm," he said, "if *I* was to ask a girl out, I'd go down to a pay phone so your mother wouldn't find out about it."

"I'm serious, Dad."

"I know you are. Okay—well, tell me, is this girl interested in you?"

"I think so."

"Does she know you're interested in her?"

"Yes."

"How does she know?"

"I hit her with a snowball."

"Oh. Sure. That usually does it."

Frank Tuttle sat back trying to hide his smile. A sweet wash of memories swept across his face. Love and commitment. Marriage and children. One of those children, halfway to a man, was asking him a question. The smile slowly faded as he realized there was something else to be discussed here besides the courting technique of teenage meatheads.

How to ask a girl out wasn't the only question on the boy's mind, but it was a good place to start.

"The first thing you have to understand about women, or girls, is that there's no rules to them. They're all different people. So what's right with one might not be right with another, you see?"

Norman had no clue.

"I could tell you all night how to win the heart of your little friend . . . what's her name?"

"Laura," Norman said.

"Laura. Well, I could tell you, and it might not work."

Norman didn't hear his dad's last sentence. He was flushed red as a rose hip, not believing he'd actually said her name out loud to his father.

Norman's embarrassment was not lost on the father, and Frank Tuttle decided to keep things easy for a while.

"Where would you take Laura?" he said.

"Roller skating, I guess. It's kinda that, a movie, or nothing around this town."

"Roller skating, that's good. Well, if I was to want a girl to go roller skating with me, the way I'd ask her would be to call her up and say, 'Wanna go roller skating with me?' "

"Dad, I'm serious."

"So am I. Don't make it difficult. Just call and ask her."

Norman had heard this tone of advice before. What it meant was *There's only one right way to do this, so do it and stop asking stupid questions.* Norman understood but wanted more. There had to be more.

Norman's dad sat back and watched him. Norman had two of his mom's good plastic-coated cards folded six ways. His knobby knee was bouncing a hundred beats a minute under the table, and he was going to chew a hole right through the side of his face if he didn't hurry up and say what was on his mind.

While Norman's dad waited for the question, he realized he had to have some answers. Pretty soon he had a couple of his own cards folded into squares. His leg was keeping time with Norman's under the table.

Finally Norman cleared his throat, "Dad, like, well . . . um, ya know, *after* you go out on a date and stuff, like, ya know, *then* what?"

There it was. Lying right in front of them. *Then what?* The two men looked at each other and the cards hit the table.

A simple fisherman with nothing on his side but a good heart and an obligation was faced with the task of passing along the combined experiences of an entire species pertaining to love, morality, biology, ideology, and disease. It was going to take a while.

"Normy, let me tell you some things about what you might be feeling lately. . . ."

And on into the night it went. Norman's mom snuck off to bed without interrupting, and it was well after two in the morning before the light in the kitchen finally went out.

"It's school tomorrow, bub. And you got a lot to think about." Frank Tuttle hugged his son, then shook his hand, and a stunned but wiser young man went up to his room.

Norman didn't sleep a wink. He lay there in the dark alternating between exhilaration and terror, with a good dose of anticipation for the days that lay ahead.

Especially tomorrow, because *boy* did he have some things to tell Stanley about.

THE ENEMY

Volleyball in gym class was a highlight of Norman's day. He was tall for his age and loved playing close to the net. His ball control was right out of the funny papers, but he did try hard and he played fair, and he had fun. But all the fun came to a halt when he jumped up to block a spike and hammered the ball back at Leonard Kopinski. Leonard wasn't paying attention and it hit him square in the nose. The kind of hit that brings instant tears and wide-eyed nosebleeds.

The blow sat Leonard right down on his butt. He held his face in two hands while the rest of the boys, in a fine display of sportsmanship, laughed at him and clapped Norman on the back.

"Hey, hey. Way to go, Tuttle!"

"Yeah! Nailed it!"

Norman started to cross under the net to help, but Coach Crawley beat him to Leonard, who would not accept any assistance. He pushed the coach away and stood facing Norman. Then Leonard pointed a bloody hand and, in a voice that sent dread reeling through Norman's skinny body, hissed, "You're dead, Tuttle."

Tuttle. He spit the word like phlegm.

"It was an accident." Norman hadn't intended to plead, but it came out that way. This wasn't wasted on Leonard, who strutted out of the gym letting his nose bleed freely. In this unwelcome bout with his earliest enemy, Norman had lost the first round.

Norman didn't know very much about Leonard Kopinski, but what he did know unsettled him. Leonard talked back to teachers and smoked cigarettes. He'd been caught stealing. Norman couldn't understand this. His parents, he was certain, would have him executed for any one of those things. Leonard had also been held back a grade somewhere, and that made him a year older. One year is an ice age of changes in junior high terms, and Leonard's lead in the physical maturity department was evident. Painfully evident to Norman, who, while taller than most boys including Leonard, was a little slower on the hormonal draw. Norman had boyishly smooth and long legs and arms while Leonard looked to be in need of a shave.

Norman soon found out that you don't have to do very much at all with your enemies. They pretty well take care of things themselves. On his way to English class from the gym, Norman ran into Leonard's two perennial sidekicks, Weird Eddie Talbot and Glenn Ferguson. Weird Eddie had earned his reputation in seventh grade when he had swallowed the principal's goldfish on a dare from Glenn, then puked it back into the aquarium. The fish survived, and Eddie became immortal. Eddie and his shadow, Glenn, were rough-looking boys like Leonard and were presently draped against their lockers watching Norman approach. Norman saw them and it made him self-conscious. His feet didn't want to work properly and he stumbled at least twice on the perfectly smooth floor. The boys chuckled and fell in beside Norman.

"You're dead, Tuttle," they declared, as if informing him he'd won the all-school raffle, and jostled him loose of a notebook before peeling away.

While he was stooped to pick up his papers, even his best friend, Stanley, got in on the action. "What did you hit Leonard Kopinski in the face for?" he said as Norman stood up. "He told the whole school he's going to kill you."

"It was an accident," Norman said helplessly.

Norman was a miserable student of English that day. In the way falling in love gives meaning to pop music, having someone out to kill you gives a special charge to a discussion of tribal warfare in *Lord of the Flies.*

I'm dead, Norman thought, feeling like a pig head on a poker.

Not even Marilee Piedmont's bra strap showing through the back of her blouse could offer him any comfort or distraction. All he could think about was Leonard Kopinski. The menace in his voice. The power in his gait. And those tears of rage in his eyes. Rage and something else. Something that chewed at Norman and soured his stomach. Something he couldn't quite identify.

As awful as English class was that day, it was still far too short for Norman's taste. Soon he was out of the protective custody of the school building and standing with Stanley Bindel waiting for the bus. Everyone else carried on with their usual after-school escapades—stomping mud, surfing ice piles—but Norman stood propped up in his big pack boots. The bleak gray patches of dirty snow reflected Norman's mood. The spring afternoon was typical of Alaska: blue and warming above, cold, dark, and oozy at your feet.

He scanned the gangs of kids for one specific face— not Laura Magruder's for the first time in months. Then Norman heard a pop in his head like a knock on a wooden door. An instant later he felt the sting and wet of an ice ball that had found him right at the temple.

In reflex and agony he clutched the side of his head, then wheeled around to see the face. There stood Leonard Kopinski sporting a grin as cold and hard as that ice ball. His arms were at his sides and his feet were set apart. Weird Eddie and Glenn stood on each side like lieutenants to their general, and all three wore the obnoxious smirks of bad boys on the high ground. They waited for a reaction.

Paralyzed with pain and surprise, Norman said nothing. He stood there with his hand to his head and did nothing. Fighting back the tears of rage, he teetered on the brink of a different kind of tears and understood then what he'd seen in Leonard Kopinski's face in the gym. It was humiliation.

To the dismay of three bad boys and one disappointed best friend, Norman Tuttle climbed onto the bus and hid his face by pretending to be looking for something in his book bag.

By the time the bus pulled away, Leonard, his friends, and at least a dozen neutral bystanders had a cruel chorus going that burned hot into the tender spot on the side of Norman's head: "Tuttle is a chicken, *baak-baak-baak* . . . Tuttle is a chicken, *baak-baak-baak.*"

Norman pulled out his algebra homework and pretended to do it, but he was thinking of only one problem, and it had nothing to do with mathematics. Norman sensed that this Leonard mess had not been concluded with his defeat. Leonard had tasted blood. Now he would want the kill.

"Norman Tuttle, what happened to your face?" In spite of his efforts to conceal it, Norman's mother spotted the blood-shot knot when Norman finally had to drop his hand to eat.

"Huh? Oh. This?" He pointed as if to make sure it was the

big red lump she meant and not some other thing. "Just a snowball fight at school."

Pretty smooth, Norman thought, just as his father shot him a look from across the mashed-potato bowl.

After the dishes were cleared and washed and the rest of the family had drifted off, Norman flipped his book bag onto the kitchen table to settle into homework mode. Norman's father sat back down opposite him, pretending to be interested in a crumpled handout about the eighth-grade graduation dance coming up in May.

"You ever get your date with that Magruder girl?" Frank Tuttle said by way of opening.

Norman glanced up at the paper. "No. I mean, not yet. I'm thinking of asking her to that." Norman nodded at the paper in his father's hands. "I don't want to rush things."

His father chuckled. "Yeah, it's only been three months. Don't get ahead of yourself."

Norman grinned, unprovoked. Talking dating strategies with his dad was the last thing on his mind. He absently fingered the lump on his temple, pulling his father's attention to where it wanted to be in the first place.

"How's it goin' at school, bub?"

Norman knew this kind of open-ended, just-asking question from his father and wasn't surprised by it. What it meant was *I know something's wrong at school and you better tell me straight.* So Norman, in his way, did tell it straight—with a question.

"Have you ever been in a fight, Dad?"

Frank Tuttle looked at his son and understood immediately. His boy was mixing it up with somebody at school. His teeth locked, and his face went red. It was unclear what was making him madder: the fact that somebody had hit his boy or that his boy might be hitting somebody else. There was nothing he despised more than violence. Growing up in a roughneck fishing port had shown him all the stupid fistfights he could stand. Two years in the army had shown him the rest. He took a long pause, trying to compose himself before answering.

"Norm, I . . . I don't know what's going on here, but . . . I guess I do know what's going on here. To answer your question, no, I have never been in a fight. Not in my life. I've had opportunities, and some might say I've had reasons"—Frank Tuttle held his meaty fisherman's hands out in front of him—"but these hands have never hit another human being, and they never will. There's no good reason why a decent person should ever use his fists. I'm very proud that I haven't. As proud as I am of anything, and you will be too when you're my age."

Norman thought of Leonard's cold sneer and wondered if he would live that long.

His dad leaned forward, ready to stand. "A man might win a

fight, Norman. But the bigger man walks away from one. So just leave it alone. As long as you live, you'll be glad you did."

And that was it. The man stood and turned. No questions from the gallery. No explanations or but-what-ifs. Norman knew when the law had been laid down. *Just leave it alone*.

His father left the room while Norman puzzled over this new information. It sounded grand, even noble. But as hard as he thought about it—and he would think about it all night long—he still couldn't figure out what he was supposed to do about Leonard Kopinski.

He was still puzzling over what to do about Leonard Kopinski when the bus pulled up in front of the school the next morning. When the doors swung open and Norman stepped out, he couldn't believe his ears.

"Tuttle is a chicken, *baak-baak-baak* . . . Tuttle is a chicken, *baak-baak-baak*." Like they'd been standing there all night long, Leonard and his cronies were posed in their same menacing T formation and chanting at him.

Norman ducked his head and tried to walk around them. Leonard stepped into his path, and Norman had to either stop or run into him. He stopped.

As the bus pulled away, the other kids gathered around, buzzing and jostling for viewing position. More students saw the action and moved in, calling out to each other.

"Fight!"

"Fight!"

"Fight—fight—fight—fight." The rhythmic chant began.

Leonard Kopinski glanced at the assembling mob, smelled the blood lust, and appeared to collect confidence.

"Why'd you run away yesterday, chicken butt?" Leonard stepped closer, looking up slightly at Norman.

"I didn't run away. I got on the bus." Norman tried to sound calm and reasonable even as his blood pounded in his ears and his knees shook.

" 'I didn't run away, I got on the bus,' " Leonard mocked, employing the universal wit of cretins young and old. Then he reached out and knocked off Norman's hat. The tender spot on the side of his head complained, and Norman felt exposed. A gasp went up from the spectators.

Norman bent down to pick up the hat and Leonard used the opportunity to push him with a big boot. Norman stumbled but kept his feet and turned again to face his attacker, pupils wide, head empty. His breaths were short and his eyes darted around the faces looking for support, an answer, a rescue . . . anything. All he saw was Stanley Bindel looking at him, then away from him. Thanks, pal.

Leonard circled around Norman, pushing at his chest. "C'mon. C'mon, chicken butt."

Norman's head was swimming. Walk away.

How do you get away?

Men win.

Big men walk.

Leave it alone.

It was an accident.

Norman didn't want to fight. Not one single atom of him did. But what he didn't realize was that he already was fighting. In the world of eighth-grade hand-to-hand combat, pushing a person around until he cries is a righteous fight. Two people pushing each other around is a real barn burner. Leonard knew this, but Norman didn't.

He'd seen Leonard push people around before and figured those had been rehearsals for the real deals, which happened somewhere else. Everyone had heard the stories of how Leonard Kopinski had kicked some guy's butt or rearranged the face on this kid from Anchorage. But Norman had never seen it. He'd only seen fights on television where people were left in heaps on the floor and thrown off cliffs, and he was scared to death.

"C'mon. C'mon, chicken butt." Norman could smell Leonard's breath as the older boy kept hammering his fingers into Norman's breastbone. "Can't fight without your volleyball, chicken butt?"

The other kids stopped chanting. Some glanced around nervously, on the lookout for teachers. Laura Magruder scuttled off to find one. Norman wasn't getting mad. He wasn't getting worried. He was getting panicked. All judgment and reason were leaving him and instinct was taking over.

His instinct told him that at any moment he was going to be hit and injured, and his reflexes took it from there. Without conscious direction or strategic forethought, Norman's long, thin arm cocked a tight little bony fist behind his back and burst forward with the sorriest roundhouse punch ever conceived. But it was a sorry roundhouse punch that just happened to land right-smack-dab-and-start-the-count on the end of Leonard Kopinski's nose.

It was a solid hit. A moment of silence that seemed like a long, harsh month hung in the schoolyard. Leonard went to his knees holding his nose, and Norman held on to his own hand.

Did I do that? How did I do that? Norman was stunned at what he'd done and surprised to find out that hitting somebody in the face hurt so bad. I think I broke my thumb, he thought.

But the harshest thing of all during that long, agonizing moment was coming up from deep inside him as he looked into Leonard Kopinski's eyes. There was no rage, no menace, no threat. Not even humiliation endured. The tears on his enemy's face were tears of pain, and Norman realized with belly-twisting shame that he'd hurt him. He looked at the manic, satisfied faces around him and began to hear their voices, one by one.

"Hey, hey! Way to go, Tuttle."

"Nailed 'im."

"Leonard is a crybaby, waah waah waah."

Stanley and the other boys closed around Norman while Leonard walked quickly away, still bleeding, still crying, his loyal lieutenants declining to go with him.

Eddie and Glenn were dazed. Norman was dazed. He could barely hear what was going on. Then Coach Crawley had him by the elbow, pulling him into the school with threats of suspension, telling him that his father would have to come down. None of it got through to Norman.

All he could hold in his mind was that forever, as long as he lived, he would be the guy who hit Leonard Kopinski. There was nothing in the world that could be done about it now, and the sting on his knuckles rang clear through him.

THE NEW-HORIZON WALTZ

In spite of his jangled nerves, Norman was enjoying getting dressed up for the big night. After grounding him for a month, his mom and dad had let him spend some of his fishing money from last summer on a brand-new coat and pants. He looked pretty sharp even if he did go through a bowline and two clove hitches before giving up and letting his mother tie his necktie.

Norman watched in the mirror with frustrated interest. "What's that knot called anyway?"

"It's a Windsor knot," she said, patting her handiwork with rough and slender fingers.

"Is it good for anything besides this?" Norman fingered the neat triangle his mother had made at his collarbone.

"Dressing up for grand occasions isn't good enough?" his mother teased.

The grand occasion was the junior high school graduation dance—made even grander by the fact that Norman had a date. A real live date of the female variety. Specifically, one Laura Magruder.

Norman and Laura's long and bashful courtship had so far been made up of stolen glances, playful snowballs, and wishful thinking. Norman found himself stricken so clueless regarding the methods of dating that it took him five months to ask her out from the time he'd decided it would be a pretty good idea. When he finally did ask her, he did it in the traditional manner: He'd written a note and given it to Stanley, who e-mailed it to Laura's friend, Marilee, who forwarded it to Laura, who punched in a long line of smiley faces, then ran it back through the pipeline. Stanley printed out the smile-laden message and handed it to Norman on the bus.

"Well, she's either laughing at you or she said yes."

Norman still had the note folded up in his wallet.

The couple had had no other communication over the past three weeks except when Marilee rushed up to Norman in the hallway one day and gushed, "Laura's wearing fuchsia to the dance if you're going to buy a corsage."

She gave Norman a stiff don't-blow-it-you-dope smile and swept back around a corner, no doubt to join Laura, who'd orchestrated the whole thing.

Norman wobbled in the hallway, flushed with the joy of contact with his beloved. Only two things were spinning through his mind: *fuchsia* and *corsage*. What the heck was she talking about?

Norman's mother was able to clear up the entire fuchsia/

corsage quandary with one straight answer, and Norman found himself the proud owner of a big pink wrist corsage of carnations and lace.

"You mean she wears this thing on her arm?" Norman held the box as if it contained a rat.

"On her wrist," his mom corrected, laughing as she placed the box back in the refrigerator.

His dad had insisted he get a pink carnation boutonniere for himself, and this might have been at the root of Norman's anxiety in front of the mirror.

Stanley's going to have guppies when he sees me. Norman was thinking of his merciless friend while appraising his reflection. If Norman occurred only in a vacuum, he would have been a sight to behold. He had a positively natty-looking navy double-breasted blazer over light gray slacks and black wingtips. He wore a light blue cotton oxford button-down shirt with a splash of color added by a red-and-black-striped necktie. His mom had picked out the whole thing during an excruciating visit to the J. C. Penney men's department in Anchorage, which was a four-hour drive and thirty-seven gentleman's-etiquette lectures away over a bad road. Maybe it had all been worth it. Everything pretty much fit, and Norman thought that if he angled his head just right and crossed his eyes, he might even be mistaken for a young Prince William.

The problem with all this self-admiration was that Norman did not occur in a vacuum. He occurred in a small town at the end of a long, rough road through Alaska surrounded by friends and associates of questionable integrity who might have a comment or two about his appearing in public looking like a royal English preppy with a pink flower stuck to his chest and a fuchsia female on his arm.

Norman suddenly felt like he was on the way not to a dance but to his sentencing hearing.

Norman was a pace or two ahead of Stanley in his adolescent development. Girls to Stanley were still a mere curiosity, while they had clearly progressed to an obsession for Norman. More and more often the boys' conversations on the bus were ending in awkward silence.

"You're bringing a *girl* to the dance?" Stanley said midway through a gummy worm, the gelatinous rainbow-colored creature still dangling from his teeth. "What for?"

Norman had no easy answer to the question. At least none that he felt Stan would not laugh at. Norman wanted to bring Laura to the dance just so he could stand near her. Breathe in her scent. Begin planning the temple of love he would build for her on top of Mt. McKinley one day. But this was not the reason he could give his friend for asking a girl to a dance. So, for Stan's sake, he toned it down. "I dunno. Hang out, I guess."

"You gonna kiss her, Norm?" Stanley teased.

"No! I mean . . . I don't know. I mean . . ."

"You think you're going to *kiss* Laura Magruder?" Stanley slurped up the rest of his candy worm and laughed with disgust.

"Shut up, Stanley," Norman grunted, and closed the subject by sliding open the window. The blast of fresh air felt good on his face, and the mingled smells of road dust, wild roses, and the green grass of spring filled the bus. Norman had a driving need to dismiss these topics from conversation because that was all he had in his head. Even the sight of two seagulls cruising for garbage over the landfill looked like romance to Norman and it had begun to unnerve him.

His poise was no better tonight as his mom snapped Polaroids of him on the way out the door with his dad. He was going to a dance with *Laura Magruder*. His Laura. The girl of his dreams and the featured attraction of a long-playing fantasy that had developed into love, marriage, fast cars, weekend getaways—and no little bit of kissing.

Norman fingered the corsage box in his hands and thought about the idea that he was going to be face to face, so to speak, with his fantasy in a few minutes. When the reality of the matter struck him, he felt a full-body sweat coming on.

He must have sucked in his breath because suddenly his dad was distracted from the driving and said a most unlikely, and unsettling, thing. "You look all grown up in that outfit, bub. A real lady's man."

And then he laughed at some private joke, put a warm hand on Norman's bony knee, and sang a line from a song Norman's mom had sung to her son at least a thousand times, but not in years. "Normy, Normy, puddin' and pie, kissed the girls and made them cry."

His dad laughed again, and Norman clutched the corsage box in white-knuckled terror.

When Laura came around the corner into the living room, Norman had a mild cerebral hemorrhage, which triggered a sort of palsy, setting his hands and knees trembling, and a cold sweat poured from his forehead and palms.

Laura had on a bright pink dress that was bunched and folded in such a way as to flatter the feminine lines of her budding form. Norman could only gawk. She looked like a . . . well, a woman. No, a queen. No, a *goddess*.

Laura blushed as bright as her dress when the elder Tuttle whistled at her good-naturedly as he stood off to the side with the proud father. Mrs. Magruder fussed between Norman and Laura, picking off lint, smoothing ruffles, and helping with the corsage, which Norman had lost all ability to manage.

"Oh, don't you look handsome, Norman. Laura, don't pick at your lace, it will snag. Frank, what happened to our babies?"

Norman's dad beamed and said, "That's what we get for feeding them, I suppose."

Laura and Norman were stood in front of the TV console to have their picture taken, and Laura lit a fire in Norman's faint heart when she hooked her arm in his for the portrait.

Norman figured it was probably four thousand degrees in the Magruders' house, and he welcomed the cool evening air across his face on the way to the car. His dad ceremoniously presented the open rear door of his mom's big dumb sedan. Laura stepped daintily around the mud holes in the driveway and got in first, sliding over only far enough to let Norman fall in close beside her. Then she had the audacity to sit there pleasantly smiling and smelling as sweet as strawberry sherbet while Norman pretty much rode the door handle all the way to the gym.

The theme of this year's graduation dance was New Horizons, so Norman and Laura had to walk into the gym through a cardboard sunset with crepe paper streamers dragging across their heads. All the basketball hoops had been filled with balloons and streamers to achieve a sort of sorry-looking carnival atmosphere. It was like a weird dream where a day at school gets all mixed together with a birthday party. Stanley Bindel's dad was the acting DJ on a raised stage made out of the lunch tables at the other end of the gym floor. He announced the couples as they pawed their way through the sunset streamers.

"And now arriving through the horizon's gate are graduates Laura Magruder and Norman Tuttle."

Laura and Norman heard simultaneous applause, insincere oohs and aahs, and laughter. As Norman's eyes adjusted to the dim light, he saw that the room was clearly divided into three approximately equal factions. There were the other couples, standing in the sheltering shadows of the bleachers. The single girls were gathered around the restroom door. And the single boys were horsing around the punch-and-cookie table.

To Norman's immeasurable dismay, the first face he chanced to focus upon was that of his friend Stanley, who jostled the boys next to him for a look. Stanley mouthed "hubba hubba" in mock admiration while the rest of the guys blew kisses and snorted.

The single girls were giving Laura no better treatment as

they looked on with mischievous smiles, talked to each other behind their hands, and bolted in twos and threes into the bathroom.

The most recently arrived duo descended into the timid throng of other couples in the shadows. When Norman's eyes got used to the still dimmer light by the bleachers, he was made even more uneasy by the sight of unbridled hand-holding, arms on shoulders, and even one occasion of lingering-on-the-lips kissing going on a little farther up the bleachers. One more nudge of his nerves and Norman might well have rattled apart.

Laura seemed comfortable enough with the whole thing as she maintained that pleasant smile on her face and stood admiring the other dresses in the room.

"Scott and Jeannette look good together, don't you think?" she said.

Norman jumped at her voice. It was the first either of them had spoken since he arrived at the Magruders' door. He looked to where she was looking and was shocked to realize that the Scott and Jeannette she was referring to were the kissing couple up in the bleachers. Norman's mind raced with panicky possibilities.

Was this a hint? Was she letting him know that kissing was okay with her? Right here in the gym? Was that what she wanted him to do? All of a sudden every one of Norman's bold and manly fantasies vanished from his head, replaced by a hot anxiety that sent his mind somersaulting so hard and far that he could scarcely contain the details of the evening.

He would only ever remember sweating buckets to dopey sixties love songs and the distinctive aroma of a gymnasium mixed with fruity perfume. This is the smell that so many fall in love to. And Norman *would* fall in love that night.

It happened, he guessed, after their second or third dance at Laura's insistence, when she declined to let go of his hand after the music stopped. The song had been "Unchained Melody."

Oh, my love . . .

Norman swallowed hard.

I hunger for your touch . . .

They walked back to the bleachers finger to palm and sat down. Everything was done in silence. It was all body language now.

Norman could see the impish Stanley making some joke and gooning at them from across the gym, but it meant nothing to him. The feel of Laura's hand in his was something just short of out-of-body ecstasy, and he would have cheerfully dropped dead on the spot if it wasn't for that very live worry about the next step. The step he felt would propel him past boyhood and fling him headlong into life's next dimension. The kissing step.

Norman sat still and quietly sweated on Laura's hand while he calculated this maneuver. He zeroed in on the location of her lips out of the corner of his eye and ran through a couple of attack scenarios. She was too far away for him to reach in one lean, so he'd either have to scoot over or trust her to meet him halfway. He couldn't risk being puckered up all by himself halfway there, so he decided that scooting over was his only alternative.

It would have to be done in one smooth motion like James Bond might do it: scooch over and swing the face around. Just like that. But then he wondered what side his nose should go on. If they both tried to go the same way with their noses, it could ruin the whole thing.

He was trying to remember from television and movies if there was a rule to that. Like if you're sitting to the girl's left, you always keep left with your nose. That would make sense, he thought. It would be the same way he was leaning. Okay, that's what he'd do. One quick scoot, a smooth swoop, and keep left.

Norman's pulse was pounding so hard it was making his ears wiggle. This was absolutely the hardest thing he'd ever tried to do, and he had to do it now.

No, on three. One . . . two . . . No, a big breath, then

on ten. One-two-three-four . . . Laura scooted over toward him and squeezed his hand tight. What's she doing?
five-six-seven . . .

"Norman?" Laura leaned her head toward his ear, and
Norman stopped the count.

"Yeah?"

Laura squeezed his hand again and said very softly, "You're
so nice. I could sit here and hold hands with you all night
long." She turned her head away and left Norman in the
intense afterglow of his first intimate experience.

It was a sweet, cool relief that washed over him when he
realized he didn't have to kiss her—that all circuits were
sufficiently loaded just the way things were. And they kept
them that way. Adjusting a grip now and then. Sending a
reassuring squeeze at calculated moments and leaning back
into the lap of an intoxicating new episode.

There was no doubt left that when Laura Magruder and
Norman Tuttle walked back through that cardboard sunset to
start their summer, it was going to be a different sort of summer
from any they'd ever seen before.

A GOOD LONG DAY

"Get your hand out of the web, Norm."

Norman was wiggling a fish out of the gill net being hauled on board by the big hydraulic drum his dad controlled from the other side.

"Norman! Watch your hand!"

The drum, looking like a fishing reel on steroids, thunked to a stop, and Norman looked up with one hand still on the fish. The other hand, he saw to his horror, loosely gripped the webbing of the net just at the point where it wrapped onto the drum. Norman snatched back his hand as if he'd been bitten.

"How many times do I have to tell you?" His dad leaned in to grab the bright silver salmon still struggling in the net. Gently he dropped it to the deck with a loose collection of identical fish from the morning's first set. "If you get your fingers wound up in this web, you're liable to lose them! C'mon, Norman, where's your head at?"

It's still in my bunk, thought Norman. It's four o'clock in the morning. The entire rest of the planet is asleep except for us and this small fleet of lunatics in Alaska out looking for fish before breakfast. And besides, for your in-formation, it's my birthday!

"I dunno," he mumbled, looking quickly to the nearby boats, afraid someone might hear his dad chewing him out. They could have heard if they wanted to. The morning was as still as sleep. The sun was already nudging over the horizon on this June 21, the longest day of the year. A normally nervous ocean surface was flat as a wet table. The towering snow peaks of the mountains across the inlet were lit orange by the rising sun and reflected double on the smooth water. Twice as beautiful on a good day. Not today.

"Stay clear of the reel, and pay attention to what you're doing!" His dad threw the large drum back into motion with a swipe at the brass hydraulic lever.

Norman took a step sideways, away from the powerful drum and toward the stern of the boat where the dripping net stretched over the rail and tailed out across the glassy water in a dotted line of floating white corks. For the last few days the gear returned after every set as a pageant of kelp, sticks, jellyfish, and an occasional sockeye salmon. Reds, they were called. Money fish. The problem was, they were only five or six pounds apiece. At a dollar per pound—and when fishing was this slow and flotsam this thick—it meant you had to haul an awful lot of web and kelp and sticks and jellyfish on board before you found a paycheck anywhere.

Norman's share of the catch was ten percent, after expenses. That was less than fifty cents for each fish. He glanced at the dozen or so fish lying around their feet. Six bucks to me, he thought. Maybe. I got out of bed in the middle of the night on my birthday for six bucks? Another fish flopped over the railing. Norman plucked it from the web and let it slap down on the deck. Six-fifty.

"Easy! You'll bruise the flesh."

Like you haven't been telling me that for four solid days, Norman thought. "It slipped," he said.

"Just do your job."

Some job. Norman ticked through his job description while he performed it. Stretch net across drum so that it spools evenly by putting hands on web. Get hands out of web. Pick fish from web. Get hands out of web. Don't bruise fish. Pick sticks and kelp from web. Get hands out of web. Pick out jellyfish before they get squeezed against the drum and explode in everyone's faces. Get hands out of web. Let's review . . .

"Nice morning, ain't it, Norm?" His dad squinted toward the rising sun, probably trying to make peace on a day that was getting off to a rocky start.

Norman thought it would be a nice day if a person wasn't on a fishing boat picking out sticks and jellyfish on his birthday before the birds were even awake.

"Yeah," he said.

"I wonder what those poor city folks are doing today."

His dad loved to say that. As if the folks back in town didn't know how bad they had it. Sleeping in. Eating hot food. Showering. Walking on the beach with their girlfriends.

Norman's thoughts took a hard turn to port, straight toward Laura Magruder. Yesterday when they'd stopped in at Port Vixen to ice the hold he'd picked up three letters from Laura. Just the smell of her perfume on the envelopes made it nearly impossible to leave the nest of sleeping bags and magazines that was his bunk and his refuge down in the fo'c'sle. He'd read the letters a dozen times each since yesterday. They were now jammed down into the end of his bunk in the very point of the bow of the boat. Ten paces from where he stood and a whole world away. But it didn't matter where they were. He had them nearly memorized.

June 14

My Norman,

I love writing that. I could do it over and over again. My

Norman. My Norman, I miss you SO MUCH!! These are the longest days of the year in every way because I have to spend them WITHOUT YOU! I won't even get to see you on your birthday. That's why I'm sending this early so maybe you'll get it in time.

I was so sad when you left the dock today. I read somewhere that it's bad luck to watch a boat disappear from sight, but I couldn't help it! I watched you all the way out of the harbor. Did you see me? I could see your dad on top steering the boat but couldn't tell if you were up there too. If you are reading this, then it means you made it to Port Vixen and picked up the mail. I will write you again REAL SOON! I have to hurry to send these before the mail boat leaves.

Happy birthday, my fisherman. My Norman. Did your dad do something special? Something dumb?

OX OX OX forever!

Laura

Norman didn't really understand the part at the end about the oxes, but the rest of it was driving him crazy in a most wonderful way. Laura actually missed him! All this time he'd been on the boat thinking about her, she'd been back in town thinking about him! He'd been so afraid that she wasn't. Now he couldn't stop thinking about the fact that Laura couldn't stop thinking about him.

It's like a vicious circle, he thought. The drum ground

slowly away at his side, the corks squealing in protest as they packed against each other. This must be what love is.

Norman saw a slimy glob glitter in the sun only out of the corner of his eye. Stinging cells in jellyfish felt like acid on the skin and could keep burning for hours, even days, leaving big red splotches and some very unhappy fishermen. It was always bad news to get sprayed by jellyfish, and it was Norman's job to make sure it didn't happen.

His left hand floated up to clear the jellyfish as he drifted toward the drum without thinking. Then it was too late to think. Norman's thumb caught under a strand of the net and was rammed hard into the confusion of webbing already stretched around the drum. Two things happened at once: the jellyfish exploded and sprayed the area like a raw egg shot through a screen door, and Norman heard something in his hand give way with a dull, nauseating pop.

"Aaagh!" father and son screamed together, turning their faces away from the spray of jelly.

"Oh for crying out loud! My eyes!" His father groped for the lever and stopped the drum. Norman was halfway over the top of it now, hanging by a thumb.

"My hand, Dad. My hand! Back off the gear!" Norman could see jelly glinting off his father's face. In his eyes.

Without really seeing what he was doing his father reversed the drum and Norman's feet came back down on the deck.

"Norman, you're getting to be as much help as two good men who stayed in town!" His dad ducked under the net and held him under the arms while trying, impossibly, to blink away the sting in his eyes. "Why didn't you clear that jelly?"

Norman had turned his face in time and only felt a little burn on the back of one ear, but he was hardly aware of that. "I broke my hand! Ow! Ow! Don't move me. My hand is caught!"

Finally his dad got the picture and frantically groped down the sleeve of Norman's rain gear until he felt the gloved hand. It was free of the pinch on the drum and barely caught on the webbing. Gently he freed the hand and pulled off the glove.

"Hold still, son!" he said, still angry for some reason.

Norman heard an eruption of excuses fly out of himself. "I was watching the net to be sure we didn't drift over it. Why didn't you see the jellyfish?"

"My job is to make sure the boat doesn't drift over the net! I'm the skipper, remember? *Your* job is to keep jelly-fish out of my face and your hands out of my net! Good God, Norman." His dad shook his head hard, like a dog trying to dry off. "Stand clear. We'll have to deal with your hand in a minute. I've got to get this gear aboard before we do drift into it." He wiped his face, uselessly, against his arm. "I'll be lucky to see for the rest of the day."

Norman's face burned like ten jellies, but not from the sting and not from the fact that his hand throbbed like a diesel. The pain brought tears to his face, but what made it sting was knowing that this time everyone crowded around the little point on this quiet morning could hear his dad hollering at him.

Two kids from Port Vixen on the nearest boat called over, "Want some peanut butter with that jelly?"

The skipper of the *Salmonater* on the other side called them by their vessel name on the sideband radio. "*Francine*, calling the *Francine* . . . How's that new deckhand workin' out there, Frank?" A trail of laughter blared out of the deck speaker before the microphone was cut.

Now the whole fleet knew he was a screw-up, thought Norman, cradling his rapidly swelling left hand.

"Never mind them," said his dad, sounding calmer now as he rapidly spooled the net in, pausing only to take out the largest sticks and clear the few fish. "Keep that hand held high. It won't hurt so much."

Once the net was aboard, Norman held the saltwater deck hose with his one good hand for his father. He trembled with pain and also fear that he could not move the thumb of his left hand at all. He kept it all to himself while watching his father viciously scrubbing his face and neck with dish soap.

"How's your eyes?"

"It's no use." His father stood up and pulled his hands away from his red, swollen eyes. "They're awfully hot this year, these jellyfish. I won't be able to see straight for hours. But I'll be okay." He wiped dry with a clean towel and took off his rubber coat. "Let's have a look at that hand now."

Norman held out his puffy left hand and winced without crying out as his father probed the joints.

"Does this hurt?"

"Yeah."

"This?"

"Uh-huh."

"How about here?"

"Ow!"

"Good."

"Good?"

"I don't feel anything broken. You popped your thumb out of joint is what you did. Happens to your Uncle Stu all the time. I swear, sometimes he can put his thumb out picking his nose!"

Norman laughed in spite of himself. "So what does that mean?"

"Means we have to put it back where it belongs."

"Does that hurt?"

"Naw," his father said, squinting through bleary eyes at

something over Norman's shoulder. "Say, isn't that the Magruder girl over there?"

Norman turned his head to look, and at the same moment his dad gave one crisp yank on his thumb. Another sickening pop resonated through Norman's skeleton and he yelped like a puppy.

"Sorry, Norm. That was a dirty trick, but it's best to sneak up on a thing like that."

Norman laughed without thinking, his eyes wide with surprise and some measure of relief. There was a noticeable lack of pressure in the still-throbbing hand.

His dad opened the hatch to the hold and dropped a deck bucket inside. "Let's ice that hand and those fish and go find a quiet place to anchor up. I think we've done enough damage for one day, don't you?"

June 15

My Norman,

It is so dull in this town! There is nothing to do without you. Where are you? I picture you out on the wide ocean and your nets bulging with fish. You and your dad are heaping your boat with fish and big $$$$$$! My Norman! The boys in town are so immature! I see Stanley Bindel mowing lawns to buy video games and candy. Geek. Even my brother, Burt, looks ridiculous working at the cannery in his little rubber rain gear. (Don't tell him I said that!)

Bon voyage, my Norman! Happy birthday again. The big one-four!

More soon. Write to me!!

OX OX OX OX

Laura

June 21

Dear Laura,

Fishing is good. Big fish, big $$$. Dad says I'm good luck. I pulled my thumb out of joint today going after a tangle in the gear. It's a good thing I caught it in time. My dad could have been hurt! He says he doesn't know what he did without me. We've hardly had time to sit down or sleep until today. Dad says we deserve a day off. A nice birthday present, but I think it was an accident. He hasn't said anything about my birthday so far. He's pretty grumpy on the boat. Has to have control of everything! Who does he think he is, the captain? Ha ha.

Dad keeps asking me what I'm thinking about! It's you. You all the time. I'm so glad to hear you're thinking about me too!

Tonight the Fish and Game is closing the area down for two days. Good timing for my sore hand, I guess. Dad says it isn't worth coming to town just to turn around and come back, so we'll be tying up in Port Vixen tomorrow. Today we're just hanging out on the anchor watching the other boats work. Lucky for us! I'll mail this when we get to port.

I love getting your letters. More later . . .
COW COW COW forever!
Norman

Norman lay absently gouging at the deck beams over his bunk with his pen. His left hand was wrapped in a stretchy bandage, stuffed in a garbage bag, and packed in a pan of ice. It had gone numb hours ago, and he pulled it out once in a while just to be sure it was still there. He could hear his dad's muffled voice from the pilothouse well enough to know he was talking to Uncle Stu on the sideband radio.

His dad and Uncle Stu had always fished the *Francine* together. This year, for some reason, his uncle had decided to lease another boat and permit and was fishing on his own. Today he was across the inlet. Fishing was good, Norman heard. His dad said they wouldn't be coming across today. Taking a day off, he said. Didn't say why.

Probably embarrassed to say why, Norman thought. *Yeah, Stu, Norman made another mess. He can't work and I can't see to stir my coffee let alone pilot a boat. Sure glad I brought him along, though. Great idea.* But his dad said nothing of the kind.

Norman heard Uncle Stu ask, "Did you give it to him yet?"

His dad's lowered voice answered, "Later. When my eyes clear up."

Give me what? Norman wondered. A clue? The boot? Another lecture?

"I can't wait to hear about it," Stu said.

I'll bet, thought Norman.

"We'll be headed into Vixen to sell what little bit we got and lay over for the closing. See you there. *The Francine,* out."

His dad had taken the day's events in relatively good humor, Norman thought. Considering that Norman had single-handedly wiped out the captain and crew before breakfast, having his dad simply say, "Go keep that hand on ice. We can use a break from each other today," and disappear into the pilothouse wasn't so bad.

But still, was that any way to treat a guy on his birthday?

June 18

Dear Norman,

You are the cutest, most mature guy I know. I can't stop looking at our picture from the dance! So handsome and strong!

I'll remember that night as long as I live! Will you?

More soon!!

OX OX OX OX OX!

Laura

Norman was looking at his copy of the same picture. He saw a red-faced freak doubling as him in an oversized sport coat standing next to the most beautiful creature on earth. The picture had them framed in front of the Magruders' television console. A flash reflected in the blank screen captured the silhouette of a broad-shouldered man off camera somewhere. His dad. Always somewhere.

June 21 (again)

Dear Laura,

I look at your picture all the time. I miss you too. Dad is starting to get on my nerves. I feel like a slave!

I guess things just get a little tense between men on a boat. I wish I was home with you, walking on the beach, looking at the sunset, all that stuff. Gotta go. The master orders me up on deck! Obey or die, slave!! Ha ha.

COW COW HORSE!

Norman

"How's the hand, Norm?" His father sat at the galley table shuffling some cards. His eyes were still bloodshot and teary from the jellies.

"Better, I think. How's the eyes?" Norman said, taking a seat across the table and gingerly laying his bandaged hand on top.

"Better, thanks. Hoo boy, that was a hot jelly! I haven't felt them like this since Stu and me were still fishing with your grandpa. I always thought it was because I had boy skin. Guess not."

Norman was reminded of the radio conversation with Uncle Stu. His dad seemed in good spirits, so he risked it. "I heard you on the radio this afternoon. What was it you were going to give me today?"

His dad smiled. "What do you think it is?"

Norman picked at the bandage. "A lecture or a whipping, I guess."

A big laugh. "When was the last time I gave you a whipping?"

"Long time."

"Ever?"

"No, never." Norman looked out the galley porthole. The boat gently rocked at anchor in the warm afternoon breeze. The other boats were a mile or two away, still scratching around for a few fish off the point. He felt his face warm at the sight of them.

"I'm sorry about this morning, Dad." Norman kept his eyes on the boats. "I wasn't paying attention."

"I know you weren't. You're usually better help than this. That's why I got so frustrated about it. Sorry I hollered at you. There was a lot going on all at once there, and you scared me. I didn't even see you were caught in the gear. If I'd missed the switch, you coulda been dragged all the way over and lost your whole hand, or an arm." His dad reached over and touched the bandaged arm lightly, then pulled back. "Scared me. That's all. Sometimes men act angry when what they really are is scared."

"And sometimes I'm thinking about other things. I don't mean to screw up." Norman squirmed on the bench.

"This wouldn't have anything to do with those three letters you've got down there stinking up the fo'c'sle, would it?"

Norman's face glowed hotter. "You can smell them?"

His dad chuckled. "Smell them? I was afraid they'd catch fire. Harry told me after he left Port Vixen he had to boil a pot of cod on the mail boat just to bury the smell of them! I'd say that girl either has a thing for you or she's trying to blow us up."

It was Norman's turn to laugh. "They are pretty smelly, aren't they?"

His dad didn't answer. He looked off into the distance, thinking of something. Norman wasn't about to turn around and get his hand popped again just to see what he was looking at. He kept his attention on his father.

It was clear the letters weren't what he wanted to talk about. "When I was about your age, your grandfather gave me something I've kept all these years."

Uh-oh, thought Norman. Here comes one of those excru-ciating when-I-was-a-boy-your-age deals. He looked intently at the tabletop, hoping the moment might pass. It didn't.

"I'd always hoped one day I'd have a son of my own who would grow up to be a young man, and one day I'd pass it along to him. Then maybe one day he'd hand it over to one of his own children. That's tradition. That's how young men get going in the world."

"Is this like the prayer book Stanley Bindel's dad gave him at his confirmation?" Norman hoped not.

"Sort of," his dad said. "I asked your uncle Stu if it would be all right with him if you and me fished together this year. I wanted to see if you were ready or not."

"Ready for what?" Norman still hoped this was all going to pass without a scene.

"Ready to get going in the world. I see by the way you handled yourself today when you were hurt that you're ready as any." His dad leaned under the galley table and pro-duced a long package covered in gift paper decorated with ducks and deer and hunting dogs. "Happy birthday, Norm."

"You didn't forget!" Norman took the package. It was heavy and he had to set it down.

"How could I forget? June twenty-first, the longest day of the year and the best day of my life. My oldest boy was born that day." His dad wiped at his seeping eyes, and Norman couldn't tell if they were jellyfish tears or not. "You going to open it?"

Norman ripped at the paper and found a rifle case inside. "A gun?"

"Not just a gun." His dad showed him the buckles on the case.

When Norman looked inside, his own eyes filled with emotion. Almost enough to embarrass himself. "Grandpa's deer rifle!" he yelled, hopping his rump up and down on the galley bench, not unlike a little kid.

"Grandpa's once. Mine for a while. Yours now. Think you can handle it?"

Norman settled down and tried to balance the rifle in his one good hand. "Oh, yeah!" he said. "Can I shoot it?"

"When your hand heals. We'll get you plenty of target practice before deer season."

"Deer hunting? I get to go hunting with you and Uncle Stu?"

His dad smiled like a benevolent king. "Providing you learn how to handle this rifle between now and then. Here, let me show you how it works."

Later that day Norman was again admiring the rifle lying in the open case. He polished it with the flannel cuff of his shirtsleeve. "Thanks, Dad," he said. "I'll take real good care of it."

"I know you will, Norman." His dad leaned against the pilothouse door grinning as though a boy with a bandaged hand and a gun was the most entertaining thing alive.

Norman looked up to his father, back down to the rifle, and out the porthole again to the distant fleet of boats all chugging toward port, and he didn't know what to say except "I wonder what the poor folks in town are doing tonight." And this time he knew what it meant.

A few hours after that, Norman tore up two letters and started another.

June 21

Dear Laura,

My dad didn't do anything dumb for my birthday. He's a little corny but knows what a guy wants. So, how do you like the taste of venison?

CAUGHT DEAD

Norman tasted the sweet cut grass of Stanley Bindel's front yard and knew he was dead. He'd taken a full burst of what sounded to be light automatic weapons fire from their neighbor, Freddie, hiding behind the trash cans by the garage.

Norman loved to die. As he counted slowly to a hundred waiting for his next life, he replayed his excellent death to himself.

He'd been running full tilt across the yard in a surprise attack on the enemy position. He hadn't seen Freddie laying for him by the garage and was a little surprised to hear the sound of gunfire and the inevitable "You're dead, Tuttle!" just as he reached his full attack stride.

Norman had leaped off his feet and loosed his grip on the plywood Thompson submachine gun. He approached the ground facedown, spread-eagled, but tucked and rolled at the last possible instant, tumbling over and over in the grass and finally coming to a halt with an agonized quiver of arms and legs.

Freddie came over holding a plastic model AK-47 behind his head and cast a long shadow across his victim.

"You've only got one life left, Norman," he said, and disappeared around the house to a new ambush position.

Norman finished counting, gathered up his weapon, and stalked off into the weeds looking for enemy movement, not really thinking about what he was doing. The rules of the game gave him two lives, and he'd only spent one. With a whole life ahead of him, Norman basked in the most lighthearted afternoon he'd enjoyed in a while.

Ever since he'd been back from fishing, his life had been all about Laura. The tendons in his thumb weren't back to normal yet and so Norman was left in town with Laura, his hand in a loose bandage and his head in the clouds. He'd hardly even spoken to his old friend Stanley, and they hadn't goofed around like this at all. It was a sunny afternoon and a late date that had gotten him involved in this game of pretend war.

He'd been expecting Laura to pick him up to watch the dirt-bike races on the beach with her older brother, Burt, and his girlfriend. They were late. He'd grown tired of waiting and started to walk up the road to meet them. Like a trail through a fairy tale, the deep pink fireweed was all in bloom along the road. Sparkling glaciers wound around the handsome mountain peaks across the bay, and the scent of mowed lawns was on the breeze.

While passing the Bindel place, Norman had seen the kids running around with toy guns and stopped to watch. Norman's brother Franky was there with Stanley and his two brothers. Freddie from down the hill brought two of his cousins from Anchorage.

It had seemed kind of cute at first. Toy guns, he thought. Bunch of kids. He'd been to the shooting range twice already with his dad. He could never go back to plastic and wooden guns after hearing the bark and feeling the buck of a bona fide thirty-caliber deer rifle. But the warm day, the smell of summer, and the trash talk had lured him in.

"The Philistines are the bad guys, Freddie," Stanley declared. "They always lose."

"Then I'll be an Ashcan guerrilla this time," Freddie said. "They kick Philistinian butt."

Norman didn't know a Philistine from a canned peach but thought he recognized the Ashcan gorilla thing from somewhere. He had to step in with an opinion.

"Philistinians and Ashcan gorillas are the same thing. They're all fighting against tourism in the Middle East by the Strongmen. Strongmen are always bad guys."

It sounded okay to the younger kids, but Stanley didn't like

Norman entering into these diplomatic talks without an invitation. "You don't even know where Philistine is, Tuttle."

"I had the same geography teacher you did, *Bindel*." Norman said his friend's last name in a way they both recognized. It said *Race you to the top of the hill, I dare you to jump that creek,* and *Do you feel lucky?* all at once. They'd been saying each other's names this way for as many summers as Norman could recall.

Now, before either of them knew what happened, it had placed them each in command of his own platoon struggling for political recognition in the world of Stanley Bindel's front yard.

"Well then, *Tuttle*, take Franky, Ted, and what's-his-name and prepare for battle." Stanley waved his short squad in behind him as he headed around the house. "Strongmen, follow me!"

With his one good hand, Norman waved his newly acquired fully automatic wooden machine gun, which had been reluctantly traded by his brother Franky in exchange for a crooked stick.

"Philistine forever!" shouted Norman to the scattering Strongmen. "General Stormin' Norman will lead his troops to glory!" And three fumbling Philistinians followed their leader into the tall grass.

Norman went at his play with a fierce abandon. His summer romance with Laura Magruder, while thoroughly absorbing, was not about laughing and running around in the weeds. He was discovering that very few things about romance were fun the way he used to understand fun. Romance was mostly about long silences, nerve-wracking hand-holding, and being together. Not actually doing anything. Just being together.

Norman certainly had no idea how to explain all that to Stanley. He was worried Stanley might misunderstand and laugh at him. He was even more worried that Stanley might understand perfectly and laugh at him.

While having an actual girlfriend had boosted his experience a little out of reach of his friend, Norman sometimes missed kicking around town with his old buddy. Stanley might still be an undeveloped third-world country of a boy by Norman's new measure, but somehow the magic of a clear Alaska summer's day had placed them together once again on the battleground of boyhood.

It felt good without thinking about it, and it was such an overpowering relief from the romantic tensions of the last few weeks that Norman forgot all about Laura and her brother. Since Norman had thought of very little else *but* Laura and her brother for over two months, this was indeed a towering event in the annals of love and war.

*   *   *

Having Laura Magruder to call his girlfriend would have been enough to let Norman die a happy young man all by itself, but getting to know her brother, Burt, and his girlfriend, Jackie, was a bonus beyond compare.

Burt Magruder was probably the most popular guy in the whole school, maybe in the entire Western world. He drove a forklift at the cannery in the summers. He was the captain or president of just about everything that moved. Burt was going to be a senior this year, and Jackie—who was a past two-time homecoming queen—had graduated last spring and was already a legend. All this coupled with the fact that Burt had his own high-rider pickup truck put him on sacred footing in the world of soon-to-be-freshman Norman Tuttle.

Burt walked with a confident stride and wore a perpetual smirk insinuating that the world was nothing more than an inconvenience. But, of course, not as big an inconvenience as his little sister, Laura, and her dork boyfriend, Norman Tuttle, were getting to be.

Norman was shocked, delighted, and terrified all at the same time on the night Laura's dad suggested that Burt and Jackie take Laura and him along on their date. Burt and Mr. Magruder got into a huge yelling match in the kitchen while

Norman and Laura squirmed in the living room. Eventually Burt's vicious tones turned into whines and whimpers before he reappeared red-faced and stormed past them to the front door, muttering, "I guess you two geeks are coming with us."

In spite of Burt's ugly mood, it had been a magical night for Norman. Jackie sat so close to Burt in the cab of his truck that Norman thought he smelled clothes burning. Norman and Laura sat a little more loosely on the other side of the cab, and nobody said very much. Burt put in a pulsating CD with more bass than a tugboat smokestack, then turned it up louder than Norman had ever heard music before. Norman's brain pounded against his skull like a balloon in a bucket, and it was almost too cool to be real.

They cruised the loop from the bowling alley down through town and around the parking lot at the state road crew's truck barn about twenty-nine times, and Norman couldn't believe that all of this was happening to him. To actually be seen in the truck of Burt Magruder, and with his own date to boot! Receiving an Olympic gold medal couldn't feel that good.

Burt and Jackie seemed anxious to be alone, so when they stopped at the bowling alley for sodas, Laura and Norman stayed inside to watch the bowlers and play video games. Later on when they went back out to the truck to check in, they didn't see anybody in the cab at first and got a little worried. But a closer inspection revealed, much to their embarrassment, why Mr. Magruder had been so insistent that Burt bring Laura and Norman along on this date.

"Do you think they're okay?" Norman squinted through the steamy window.

"Oh yeah," said Laura, leading him firmly away by the hand.

And there had been many dates since then. Norman had probably been around the cruise over five hundred times so far this summer. But there had also been softball games, movies, dances, and even one bonfire on the beach when Burt drove his truck right up to the fire with the music exploding out the doors while they all climbed down.

Norman and Laura were almost universally ignored by the older kids, but they were perfectly happy just to be along and to be together. They were content holding hands off by themselves in some shadow or corner, overhearing conversations, and absorbing vital information like two sly spies in the enemy camp.

The most important thing to keep straight was the hierarchy of vehicles. Burt's big-wheeled truck ranked right up near the top, but there were several other cars and trucks that fell in and out of grace depending on the mood of the gang.

Laura and Norman soon learned which cars it was cool to admire and which ones to ignore.

"Bobby lowered his Civic."

"Mark raised his Jeep."

"Did you see Janet's new four-by-four?"

"It's her mom's Subaru."

"Sorry."

Overall Norman and Laura were learning the necessary rules of getting older. It was trickier than it looked. Because of Burt and Jackie's rather unnerving habit of wandering off by themselves, the younger couple had ample time to rehearse their grown-up talk as well as sparkle with the electricity of being close to each other.

All of this had the effect of drawing Norman into a world away from the one he had grown up in. It made him quiet at home and absent from the neighborhood. He still worked with his dad on the fishing boat between trips, and he generally spent his days doing assigned chores around the house before retreating to his room. In that solitude he found the comfort of his thoughts and the obsessions they held.

He saw Laura at least two or three times a week and talked to her on the phone every day. More and more Laura was becoming Norman's only interest in the world, mostly at the expense of his old friend Stanley.

One sunny Saturday they'd been riding around with Burt when Norman spotted Stanley Bindel with a group of other kids skateboarding on a side street. Norman was glad his old buddy would see him in Burt's truck, and he let his frame droop a little into the seat in order to deliver his most non-chalant wave.

He never made the delivery, though, because just as he was about to wave, Laura straightened up next to him and sniffed with rare viciousness, "Look at those losers playing with their toys."

Laura looked away with such purpose that it distracted Norman and left him in a helpless moment of confusion. And a moment was all it took for the truck to roll by his friend. There was nothing Norman could do but memorize the look on Stanley's passing face. It was a look like surprise all mixed up with hope and asking for mercy. It was a look that wanted the simplest thing, like a friendly wave from an old buddy.

"Hey, Stanley's okay," Norman said, jumping late to his friend's defense, then immediately regretted his tone. "He lives just up the road from us," he added, as if needing to explain how he'd even come to know such a loser. "But he can be okay," he repeated with less conviction.

Laura said nothing more. Norman sat numb, looking straight ahead, and let Stanley disappear behind him. Laura relaxed again beside him, and Norman was pulled back into the present by her touch.

He looked at Burt's irritated smirk and Laura's indifferent reserve, and he recovered himself. He was riding in one of the hottest rigs in town with the soon-to-be president of the senior class on their way to pick up the legendary Jackie while in the company of his very own girlfriend. Did he have anything to be unhappy about? Nothing he could remember.

He was crouched in the tall weeds eyeing three of Stanley's troops, who were defending the tractor-tire sandbox that served as enemy headquarters. Norman had lost the rest of his platoon already. He'd made poor choices from the beginning, and the little kids he had on his flanks were quickly ambushed and eliminated by the Strongmen.

It was just him now, and he figured he could try another suicide run at Stanley's troops. They wouldn't expect it twice from the same place. He didn't see Stanley anywhere but expected he was out back looking for him. Norman had put some thought into this, and he felt cocky enough to try it. The three defenders were looking the other way, and it was now or never.

Norman gripped his machine gun, took three deep breaths, and burst from the edge of the weeds in a silent streak toward the sandbox. His heart pounded with blood lust and the revenge that was to be his.

Just as he was about to open his mouth with deadly fire, he was interrupted by a staccato burst of verbal gunfire. "Dow! Dow! Dee-dee-dee-dow!"

It was Stanley from behind the front stairs. He'd been ambushed again.

Norman knew it was his last life and wanted to put everything he had into it. He clutched his chest and turned around. He staggered, landed on his back, and rolled. Being careful of his banged-up hand, he collapsed onto his belly, shivered, and died.

"Lame death, *Tuttle*." Stanley stood over his dead friend but was looking at a tail of dust down the road.

Norman kept his face in the grass. "I die better than you seven days a week."

Stanley backed up in the yard, away from the road. "Bet you can't do it again, *Tuttle*."

"You want it again?" Norman climbed to his feet, all tooth and grit, as he charged straight at his friend. "This is how you die, *Bindel*!"

Stanley raised his wooden carbine and fired. "Dow! Dee-dee-dow!"

Norman leaped into the air. He let fly the machine gun. His arms clutched at his guts as he turned in midair for the landing. His eyes opened, and somewhere between being gut-shot and hitting the ground, he saw that a new player had entered the battlefield.

Standing stock-still on the road in front of him was the

hottest rig in town with the soon-to-be president of the senior class, the legendary Jackie, and his very own girlfriend. Three heads turned precisely toward him with the deadly aim of a firing squad.

He caught a round each of Burt's smirk, Jackie's bored amusement, and Laura's appalled gape before he turned and fell face-first into the lawn.

Norman Tuttle tasted the grass of Stanley Bindel's front yard for the second time that day and felt a foot in the middle of his back.

"That's how you die, all right." Stanley chuckled. "See you around, *Tuttle*."

Norman slowly and hopelessly began counting to a hundred.

YOUNG BUCKS

Norman didn't want to be there the moment his feet hit the snowy beach. When he'd been asked along, deer hunting with his dad seemed like the high road to glory. But he was having a change of heart. There's something about the look of thin, wet snow on a gray November beach that can make a guy wish he were back home curled into a warm spot on the sofa in front of the tube. Or, better yet, curled up next to his girlfriend in front of the tube.

"Grab the tent and the rifles, Norman. We'll camp just inside those trees." Norman's dad walked ahead with a pack slung across each shoulder. Uncle Stu was taking some other bags and bundles out of the skiff and laying them in a neat pile on the beach.

Norman peered out to their fishing boat—so familiar and warm—anchored peacefully in the protected little cove. "Uncle Stu, why can't we sleep on the boat?"

His uncle understood but challenged him with a smile. "The key to deer hunting is to be where the deer are, my good man. The deer are in the woods, not the water. Grab those rifles like your dad said. The sooner we get situated, the sooner we can get a fire goin'."

Norman followed his dad's footprints up the beach into the trees and tried to look forward to something. It was a great honor to be along on this excursion. His dad and his uncle had been coming over for this deer hunt on Stridalof Island every year since he could remember. They would always come back three days or a week later with whiskers on their faces and deer strung up the mast, hanging proud like feathers on a warrior's lance.

Norman had only a passive attraction to hunting. He'd whacked his fair share of birds and squirrels around the neighborhood with his pellet gun, and two years ago he and Stanley Bindel had actually brought down a rabbit with Stanley's twenty-two. But there was no real passion to it—it was just something to do at the time.

Norman's interest in hunting had grown a hundredfold on his birthday, when he was presented with the thirty-thirty lever-action Winchester his dad had hunted with since he himself had been a kid, and his dad before that. It was a bush-beaten old club of a rifle, but it was a real rifle, and it was his. He had shown it off to Stanley, mostly to bug him. He'd bragged about it to Laura. His dad had taken him out to the gravel pit for target practice several weekends during the summer and fall, and Norman had even become a passable shot.

Two big nails had been pounded into his bedroom wall, and the rifle had hung there importantly ever since. He liked the look of it. He liked what it could do.

Bang. Bang. In his fantasy, a deer charging through the brush folds up and dies in a heap at his feet. *Bang. Bang.* Two deer, side by side in a meadow, drop one after the other. Dad and Uncle Stu look on. High fives, and then back to town with Norman's deer the only ones strung up in the rigging.

"The kid can shoot," his dad would say. "The kid sure can shoot."

Norman ran the cleaning rod in and out of the barrel and watched his dad check the stew pot over the fire. The smell of it stirred an empty place in his belly, and the fire felt good on his face.

His dad took a taste of the stew and nodded. "Normy, you're about to get your first taste of my world-famous camp stew."

"You'll soon discover why your mother does all the cooking around your house." Stu pounded the last of the tent stakes into the half-frozen duff surface of the small clearing and winked at Norman through the smoke. Norman grinned back and continued cleaning his rifle.

He was feeling better about things. The stew bubbled like lava, and he smelled meat and onions and wood. The tent was pitched square in the firelight, imposing order upon the wilderness. Their cozy camp had already taken away most of his chill and all of his apprehensions.

The campfire had a hypnotic effect on Norman, like nature's own channel surfing. There was nothing all that good on, but he couldn't look away. The flames bending around log and pot. The smoke spiraling up into the dark night. Their three faces shining like coins.

"This stew tastes worse than last year's." Uncle Stu was taking a big drink from his tin cup.

"It *is* last year's." Norman's dad sat on his haunches and talked to the fire.

Norman just ate his stew and listened. He loved the way grown men teased each other. They sounded so serious all the time, never laughing out loud or taking offense. Seeing the rough faces of his dad and uncle lit in the fire's glow and listening to them jab at each other gave him a comfort he'd never felt around them in town.

With nothing but the wide world of autumn all around, the fire put them in the same small room together. He saw his gun glimmering at his side, and a sense of irrepressible *manliness* came over him. Norman sat and listened to the men and poked at the fire, and he was now glad he came.

*   *   *

Norman woke to the loud blue luminescence of a nylon tent in the bright sunshine. He was alone in his sleeping bag between two other empty ones, and he scrambled out into the morning. Uncle Stu was tending to a huge cast-iron pan sitting in the fire. In it an armada of eggs and bacon floated in a solid inch of boiling oil. A pot of coffee steamed away on a flat rock to the side, and the smell of it all on top of the fine morning was a glorious thing.

The gray gloom of the day before was lost to the blue sky and low-slung November sun. The warm light silhouetted their boat still at anchor off the beach and coaxed steam off the rocks and gravel, warming Norman more by its look than anything he felt. The light wet snow was frozen crisp from the cold night, held still as a photograph to the bare branches of birch and alder and crunchy as candy frosting on the spruce trees.

Uncle Stu looked up from his greasy work at the fire. "Good mornin', Norm. Soon as your ol' man gets back we'll have us some of this fine camp breakfast. It'll stick to your ribs all day—that is, if it don't slip right through you."

Norman laced up his boots and wandered off into the trees for his morning business. When he returned to camp, his father was dishing out the dripping eggs and bacon into three tin plates.

"These are what we call *sliders*." His dad handed over a

plate to Norman. "You don't have to chew. Just suck 'em down."

Norman smiled and enjoyed his breakfast more than he had enjoyed one in a long time.

"Good eggs," Norman said between gulps.

"Have some bacon with your grease, Normy." His dad pointed at the pile of bacon with his fork. "You're still forty or fifty years from your first heart attack."

Norman laughed and felt like he was truly with the older men, not just brought along. They all laughed. They all ate.

The men talked about the day's hunt as they cleaned their plates in the gravel. His dad had been out scouting the nearby trails, and he had a plan. "There's nothing in the lower clearing, but they're around. You can see they're around. Stu, I think you and I should head up on top from east and west and let Norman stand the clearing. They might head through there on their own, but if we spook some up top, they'll come down that way for sure."

Norman didn't know exactly what they were talking about, but he was pleased to be a part of the plan and anxious to get started.

"You might be sittin' a long time today, bub." Norman's dad stuffed a day pack with a thermos of coffee, some candy bars, and a wool blanket.

Norman followed Uncle Stu's lead and loaded his rifle,

careful to leave the chamber empty like his dad had taught him. *Never leave a round in the chamber, and never pull the trigger until you're sure of your shot.* He'd heard it a hundred times at the shooting range, and he was pretty sure he knew what it meant.

The weight of that responsibility felt good slung onto Norman's shoulder as he marched up the trail between the older men. All the talking had stopped as soon as they left camp, and nobody needed to announce that they were hunting now.

He could see his dad's walk change. His feet landed differently, smoothly, and his hands reached out and guided branches and twigs quietly around him. Norman affected the seriousness of the men and tried to ape his dad's movements. The game trail they followed was covered with a partly frozen mat of wet leaves. It muffled their footfalls and gave a little under Norman's boots. Their breath puffed white in the chill and glimmered in the patchy sun filtering through the spruce canopy.

Every so often one of the men would stop and look at some droppings or tracks on the path, and Norman would watch them searching through the brush and trees for signs of deer. It was very exciting, and Norman could feel the adrenaline pumping in his chest and his attention riveting itself to the forest.

It was as if his natural senses were being cranked up brighter than he'd ever known. He was dialed in. He noticed a squirrel run up a tree trunk far, far away. He'd jump and wince at the scolding of other squirrels they passed by. He knew their position was being broadcast through the woods, and as quiet as they were trying to be, he figured they must sound like a Mardi Gras parade to any deer who lived in this kind of peace every day.

"This is where you'll roost, Norm."

Norman's dad talked in a low voice and pointed to a log lying in the tall brown weeds that made up the edge of a pocket meadow no bigger than a high school gymnasium. They had climbed a small distance and were now on a flat bench of land that interrupted the steady upward climb of the hillside.

"This is where they like to come sometimes. You sit here and watch. If you see your buck, take the shot. But be patient. We'll work our way up each side of the ridge and see what's up there."

His dad gave him one long look and patted his shoulder. Norman stood still in the gathering silence as the two men separated and headed in their different directions. The spare fall woods seemed to swallow them up as soon as they'd gone. He could mark their progress for a little while by the occasional chattering squirrel, but even that was soon lost to the drip-drop of yesterday's light snow being chased off the trees by the sun along the edges of the open meadow.

It was as quiet as a forest could possibly hold itself. Norman searched through it with his eyes and ears fully open. There was the sporadic dull *clump* of a spruce cone falling. The tick of the squirrels in the branches busying themselves with whatever it is squirrels do. And most of all there was nothing. Some dripping, and nothing at all.

Suddenly chilled from sitting still, Norman quietly unpacked his blanket and wrapped it around himself. He poured some steaming coffee, which he didn't particularly enjoy, but the company of it was good. It reminded him of the camp and the fire, and what he was doing. He wished Laura could see him sitting here.

He held his rifle between his knees and peered through the weeds. It slowly became clear that deer hunting was a lonely business. Watching. Listening. Imagining his narrowed gaze zeroing in on the prey. *Bang. Bang.*

Norman didn't know how long he'd sat there. He hadn't been asleep. He knew that for sure. But he hadn't actually been awake either. Wherever Norman had been, he hadn't been watching the meadow, because when next he noticed it, he wasn't the only critter in it anymore.

Right in front of him, not fifty feet away, stood a young buck indifferently rubbing its backside against an old fallen tree trunk. Norman almost did have his first heart attack, and his rifle found its way up into both hands. His first instinct was not the hunter's kill reflex, though. He felt something more like surprise, even delight.

He couldn't help but smile at the sight of a deer scratching its butt. Not quite the opinion he'd held of this noble beast: a big-chested animal full of defiance showing its proud antlers atop a grassy knoll in perfect outline against a scenic mountain backdrop. That's how they all looked in *Alaska* magazine. They weren't leaned over into a log with a lip curled back in the exquisite relief of getting an itch scratched. And this one didn't have any antlers at all to speak of. Only a couple of little forked horns.

Norman thought, This is just a boy deer.

Suddenly the deer sprang up like it had been called to attention. Norman watched, fascinated with this bird's-eye view of a wild animal's private moments. For no apparent reason the young buck jumped into the air, lowered its head, and charged the log it'd been rubbing. Its head hit with a hollow thud, and it staggered back a step or two before regaining its posture.

It was playing a silly battle game with itself, and Norman's snicker slipped out before he could catch it. The deer froze in place and fixed its gaze square on Norman. He looked at the deer. Two young bucks in the woods with nothing to do.

The moment was interrupted by a distant popping sound, then another like it. The reports rolled down from the ridge and echoed through the woods. It filled Norman with a grim and immediate sense of purpose.

Dad and Uncle Stu, he thought. They must have found something. He stood up without thinking, and the young deer bolted across the meadow away from him. Before Norman knew it he'd snapped the lever open and shut on his rifle, ramming a round into the chamber. The sharp sound of it somehow stopped the young buck in its tracks, and it looked back over its shoulder at the boy.

And Norman looked at the deer. Only this time it was with one eye down the barrel. It was a long, long look. He didn't know who was pulling the trigger when the gun jumped in his hand and left him and the deer standing in the inflated silence that a rifle shot leaves. A sound like a chord on a church organ. *Never pull the trigger unless you're sure of your shot*, his dad had said a hundred times.

And for a long and hopeful moment Norman had missed. The deer looked at him. Then Norman saw the hole and his breath fell out of him.

The deer broke off its gaze without turning. It just stopped seeing. It flopped down on the butt it had been scratching a minute ago. Its forelegs began to buckle, and the two forked horns fell through the weeds. The blood drained from Norman's face as quickly as it did from the deer's heart, and their heads hit the ground together.

DARK KNIGHT

The first morning back to school after a long, dark, and dull Christmas break was a festival of noise and commotion. It was a Wednesday that hung heavy like a Monday. Doors slammed and shoes squealed on the freshly rewaxed floors. Teachers hollered. Seniors strutted. Girls shrieked at smuggled snow stuffed down their collars. Insulated boots clunked into lockers with heavy coats stuffed in behind. Through it all waded Norman, scouting the crowded hallway like a lost dog.

He was suffering withdrawal. Not from his fellow students. Certainly not from school. The empty spot in him could be filled only by Laura Magruder.

"If you look to your right, you'll catch a glimpse of a rare northern love zombie," a passing Stanley Bindel commented to no one in particular. Norman ignored him and wandered on, his eyes flicking from face to face.

At last, there she appeared around the corner—that hair, those eyes, that walk. That walk that walked right by him.

"Laura! Hi!"

The love of his life pulled her attention away from whatever she was saying to Marilee Piedmont close at her side and laid those eyes on Norman.

"Oh, Norman, hi!" she said as casually as if she'd seen him an hour ago, even though it had been over a week. Even though they'd seen each other only once during the whole vacation. Even though most of his phone calls had been answered by her mother with the promise of a return call that never came.

"Where you been all week?" he asked.

Laura did not slow her stride, and Norman had to reverse direction and scamper to keep up as she said breezily, "I've been really busy."

"Still doing the house-possum training course?" Norman didn't even try to contain his agitation.

"Yes," she answered dryly. "We were taking baby-sitting classes all last week, and now we're certified!" Laura patted her book bag as if that proved it. "Marilee baby-sat for the Storbocks on Saturday night and guess who I've got for Friday night?"

"Me." It came out before he realized how it would sound. "I mean, I thought we always went bowling on Fridays."

"Not this Friday. I'll be at the Flannigans' making *five dol-*

lars an hour!" Laura held five fingers up to his face. "That's what certified baby-sitters are getting these days."

"They give certificates for that?" Norman couldn't help being snide. After being the designated baby-sitter in his household for the past two years, it was the least glamorous occupation he could imagine. Besides that, Norman could make hundreds, sometimes thousands of dollars on the boat during the peak salmon season, and so five dollars an hour was a ridiculously small amount of money to him. "Why bother?"

Laura stopped. Not to address Norman more clearly, but because she'd reached her classroom door. "Because I want to," she said cheerily, and turned into the room.

"See you in study hall?" he ventured.

"Sure."

Laura disappeared into freshman English while Norman wandered up the hall to American history. They would start the second semester with the Civil War, Mr. Bietter informed them.

"The primary aim of President Lincoln was to preserve the Union at all costs," he began. "The Confederates, however, had something else in mind. The Southern states wanted to govern themselves."

Norman looked out the window into the still-dark morning. Snowflakes hit the glass, then slid slowly into oblivion.

His mood followed them down as the clouds of war formed on Mr. Bietter's blackboard.

"Is it about me or the money?" Norman asked before he was even fully seated beside her.

"Is what about you or the money?"

"This baby-sitting thing."

Laura looked at him, genuinely puzzled. "Norman, what is your problem?"

"I'm just saying—well. I've been missing you. And. Well. If it's money you need—ya know, I've got money."

The puzzlement cleared from her face and was replaced with annoyance. "Have you ever heard of male chauvinism?"

"Is that like when knights in shining armor rescue damsels in distress?" For a moment Norman thought this thing was going his way after all, but Laura's hard look said it wasn't.

"That's chivalry. Almost the same idea. Male chauvinism is when men think they're the only ones who can do things."

"Did you learn this in baby-sitting class?" Norman sneered.

Laura ignored the comment and a chilly silence took over the moment. Norman could see he was losing major ground and softened his act.

"What *do* they teach in baby-sitting class?"

Laura braided and unbraided her hair alongside her face as

she answered, "Just a bunch of dumb stuff about fire exits and smoke alarms. The twenty-seven different kinds of household poison. How to save kids from choking. Regulate television. Stuff like that."

"The best thing to do with the TV is to turn it all the way up so you can still hear it over the crying and fighting." Norman wasn't joking. He'd put in his time with the Three Creepies, and he knew the Flannigan tribe would be no different.

A smile came to her face. "You're funny." Laura pressed his leg with hers under the table and lit him up. "I just wanted to get the certificate so people will hire me. I could make an extra twenty or thirty dollars a week!"

"For what?"

"For whatever!" Laura was getting peeved, but a forlorn look from Norman softened her again. "I'll miss you Friday night."

"It's not too late to cancel, is it?" Norman answered her leg with his knee.

"You can call me," she said sweetly, then laughed, remembering something. "They gave us a list of the top ten rules for baby-sitters. Want to know what number one is?"

"Untie the children before the parents get home?"

"That's number four," she joked. "No, it says in big block letters at the top of the handout: NO BOYFRIENDS."

"Figures."

"But I'll be all alone after the kids are asleep," she said in a teasing voice, gathering up her books to go. "You can call me."

"See you after school?" Norman touched her hand.

"Can't. Sorry." Laura stood. "Marilee wants to show me the leather coat she's saving for. I'll see you tomorrow."

Laura turned and left the room, looking back once, leaving a smile to take with him. He did—that and one other thing she'd said: *I'll be all alone after the kids are asleep.* The Flannigans' house was only a mile from his. Their kids were about the same age as Norman's brothers and sister. No boyfriends? We'll see about that, he thought, and wandered down the hall to solid geometry class.

Even Norman wasn't quite sure how he ended up hand-delivering pizza to the Flannigan home that Friday night.

All he knew was that the first time Laura called, she sounded calm enough. She made a point of saying she was calm, Norman knew, because that was rule two, right after NO BOYFRIENDS: above all, stay calm.

"Norman, hi!" she said too cheerfully. "How are you?"

"Laura!" Norman tried to sound surprised. "How's it going over there?"

"Oh, fine." He heard wailing in the background. "It's not

that I'm worried, really, but I am curious about something. I'd call my mom, but you know how parents are. She'd freak out and come over, and if the Flannigans find out, I'm finished. Anyhow, I'm wondering, um, can four-year-olds scream themselves to death?"

"I don't think so," he said, "but maybe you should call your mom or Marilee."

"I can't do that!" She no longer sounded calm. "If word gets out that I can't handle these kids, the Flannigans will never hire me again! You know they're moving to Oregon, and Mrs. Flannigan leaves in two weeks to start her new job. They'll need a lot of baby-sitting until the rest of them go."

Norman knew this was true. It was a small town. Performance mattered. "You can trust me," he said. "So, how long has he been screaming?"

"Almost an hour. He's really turning colors."

"He's old for this, but are his pants wet?"

"No."

"Check for poop?"

"Yep."

"Is he bleeding anywhere?"

"Nope."

"Burned?"

"Uh-uh."

"Pinched?"

"Don't think so."

"Good. He'll get hoarse pretty soon and quit." Norman sounded every bit the voice of experience, and it had its effect. Laura thanked him, kissed into the phone, and hung up.

Phase one complete, thought Norman.

In the second call she sounded a little more tense but still in control.

"You're right. Corey can't scream anymore, but he still hasn't stopped trying. Norman, is it true that kids can get scurvy from crying too much? And is it true that a Flintstones vitamin and a cup of hot cocoa will cure it?"

"Where'd you hear that?"

"Eddie, the oldest. He says that's what's wrong with Corey. Missy said it's true, but I don't think she even knows what scurvy is. In fact, I'm not sure I know what scurvy is."

"It's a lack of vitamin C, I think. Sailors used to get it. I don't think crying kids do. Give him the vitamin for the heck of it, but the cocoa is a trick."

Laura hung up with a grateful smooch. He lay back on his bed and bounced a Nerf ball off the ceiling with a satisfied smile. Everything was going according to plan, he thought, although the scurvy thing was a little over the top. He wished Eddie would tone it down before Laura got suspicious. He also worried that his plan might not be safe in the hands of a nine-year-old. Bribes had gotten him this far, but it might take threats to keep things under control.

"Norman?" By the third call Laura sounded rattled. "They absolutely will not go to sleep. Eddie says it's because they all have superactive thyroids, and they need food, like pizza. It can't be true, but they won't get off it. What do I do? If the Flannigans come home and they're not in bed, it's all over!"

Now Norman was really annoyed with Eddie. Superactive thyroids? He tried to put it aside for the moment and maintain his calm, steady demeanor. "What time are the Flannigans due home?"

"After midnight, they said. They're at the Elks turkey shoot."

That usually went until after two in morning, Norman knew. His parents went every year. "It's just ten now. There's plenty of time. Eddie hangs out with my little brother over here all the time. I think I can handle him. Why don't you put him on the phone." Norman liked the way he sounded.

"Here's Eddie," Laura said. "I gotta go get the battery from the TV remote out of Corey's mouth."

"Wud'ya want, kissy-face?" Eddie came on the line.

"Cool it, you little freak." Norman lowered his voice. "Can Laura hear you?"

"She's in the bathroom with Corey. I told her to hold his head underwater. He'll spit it out then."

"Very funny, psycho. How did you get him to cry so hard for so long?"

"I kept twist-pinching him when no one was looking," Eddie said proudly. "What did you think of my scurvy and thyroid?"

"I think you read too much. Listen, I paid you twenty bucks to wear her down and beg for pizza. Don't be so smart about it. Just be yourself—a jerk."

"Hey, smoochie, how would you like me to tell Laura you sleep with her picture under your pillow?"

"How'd you know that?" Norman said, going dry in the mouth.

"Your brother told me."

Norman made a mental note to murder Franky at the earliest possible opportunity. Eddie wasn't done.

"And how would you like me to tell Laura how you paid me to mess her up over here?"

Norman felt a chill and said weakly, "She'd never believe you."

"She believed the scurvy. She'll believe anything."

"Okay," Norman sighed. "What do you want?"

"The pizzas, at my door, in twenty minutes."

"Deal."

"And twenty more bucks."

"Twenty more?" Norman tried to shout and whisper at once. "That's ex . . . extro . . ."

"It's called extortion," Eddie noted calmly. "And here comes Laura now." Eddie moved his face from the receiver, "Hey, Laura, guess what Norman's trying to do?"

"Okay, it's a deal!" Norman hissed.

Laura's voice came on the line. "What's a deal?"

"Oh, Laura! Hi! Um, how's Corey?"

"He spit out the battery when I plugged his nose," she said wearily. "Now he's crying again. What's going on with you and Eddie?"

"Nothing." Norman paused to gain his composure. "I was just trying to help. I told him that we had two deluxe pizzas in the freezer and I *might* bring them over if he agreed to help you get his brother and sister to bed before their parents got home. I mean, if you want me to."

"What about the kids at your house?" she said, meaning yes.

"I've already bribed them, er, settled them down with a pizza of their own, two videos, and ice cream bars. It's in the bag. I'm only a ten-minute walk up the road. I won't be gone long. . . . So?"

A mournful cry came from somewhere in the background. "Hurry," she said, and the line went dead.

* * *

It was a deep, dark Alaska January night, and still Norman's frigid march through the wind and snow with a frozen mini-pizza under each arm warmed him like a walk on the beach. Just when he'd thought that Laura was drifting away from him, here he was. Soon enough he would be alone with his girl. This was far better even than their regular bowling date, where they were together but never alone. There were always friends at the lanes, a brother in the truck, and a parent in the next room when they returned home.

When he crunched up the front path, light suddenly fell across the ice and snow, and there she was—Laura, silhouetted in the door frame like a portrait of a tortured saint. His damsel in distress.

"Remember," Norman began, seeing the caution on her face, "I'm not a *boyfriend* tonight. I'm more like a co-baby-sitter. A consultant. You're not doing anything wrong."

"It feels wrong," she said, letting him in anyway.

"It's not," Norman said convincingly as he followed her into the warm house.

Twenty minutes and an oven buzzer later, Norman was at the Flannigans' kitchen table happily dishing out hot pizza to three sagging kids while Laura looked on nervously.

"They were supposed to be in bed hours ago," she said.

"Don't worry. This'll put 'em right down. They've about had it anyway." Norman laid out the last piece and let the sound of his voice hang in midair. It sounded good to him. There was something authoritative about it. Something . . . manly. He looked at Laura, and she'd heard it too.

"You really shouldn't be here," she said. "What if the Flannigans come home early?"

"They *never* come home early." Norman moved across the kitchen toward her.

The kids grew quiet around the pizza like a pack of wolves on a fresh kill. There was a little bit of horsing around, and goony looks from Eddie, but with no spirit to them. Norman had slipped the extra twenty under his plate, and that seemed to close the deal.

Missy, innocent of everything, finished one slice and started drooping in her chair. Looking near collapse himself, tearstained Corey picked all the pepperoni from his piece and chewed mechanically.

Laura and Norman stood off to the side like proud parents. They looked at each other, and in an instant the fantasy passed between them. Their cheeks reddened, and they averted their eyes.

It was strange to be alone in a house with kids. Their hands found each other, and they stood like that—just watching. Before long the kids would be in bed. Norman knew he'd be asked to leave, but he would not, and that would be okay. *I'll be all alone after the kids are asleep*, she'd said.

Oh no you won't, he thought, and everything he'd done to get them here seemed worth it, even noble somehow. He'd felt them growing apart, and now they seemed closer than ever before. Norman was impressed with himself. So impressed that he never even heard the car pull up.

"What on earth is going on here?" Mrs. Flannigan stood poised in the doorway with her grim-faced husband peering over her shoulder. "What are the kids still doing up?"

In an instant she was storming through the room, and it was clear she wasn't waiting for answers. "Edward Junior, Missy, Corey. Up those stairs this minute. Get those teeth brushed! Look at this house! It's a mess! Where'd this pizza come from? Norman Tuttle, what are *you* doing here?"

Then she turned on Laura and let the air out of everything. "Laura Magruder, I'm so disappointed in you. How could you let this happen?"

Laura could say nothing. Norman made eye contact with Eddie, who was palming a twenty-dollar bill on his way up the stairs. *Don't you say a word.* He beamed the thought like a laser before Mr. Flannigan turned him toward the door and gave him a firm push between the shoulder blades.

While the real man of the house was showing Norman the way out with a look like twenty-seven kinds of household poison, the boy took the briefest look back at his girl. She could only look at her shoes and fold around herself, and there was just Laura in there to face the music. No Norman, and nothing he could do.

The walk home was slow and dark. His coat flopped open in the wind, but he was oblivious to the cold. Twice he stopped and turned. He should walk right back there and tell the Flannigans what he'd done. Twice he didn't do it. A third time he might have, but then a pair of headlights came up the road behind him, casting his shadow far out ahead. The car coasted to a stop beside him, and Mr. Flannigan rolled the window down.

"Need a ride?" he said.

"No sir. Thanks. It's not far."

"Get in, Norman."

"Yes sir."

Norman climbed into the other side, but Mr. Flannigan made no motion to drive. Instead he reached his fist over to Norman and opened it. Two crumpled twenty-dollar bills dropped onto his lap.

"I found these under my boy's pillow, and you know, I got curious." The man's voice sounded friendly, but Norman wasn't that dumb. It also sounded steady and deep—like a long fall. "He's got quite a tale about this evening, and I'd like to hear your version."

Norman could not speak.

"So would your friend, who is cryin' her head off in my kitchen." Mr. Flannigan put the car in gear, and Norman watched silently as the headlights swung back toward his damsel in distress.

"What about my brothers and sister?" Norman finally asked helplessly.

"So *now* you're worried about them?" Mr. Flannigan laughed in disbelief. "I've already called the Elks. Your folks are on their way home now."

Norman watched a puff of snow blast across the road, and it was as if it passed through his own chest.

Mr. Flannigan noticed his tremor.

"Stop worryin' about yourself, Norman," he said as they pulled to a stop in front of the house. "Go in there and do the right thing."

When Norman got out of the car, the two twenty-dollar bills fell onto the snow at his feet. Eight hours' worth of baby-sitting. The calculation crossed his mind as he stepped over them toward the house knowing this was going to cost him a whole lot more than that.

A BUMP IN THE ROAD

Norman sat in the rear seat looking at the back of his father's head, waiting. His dad was going to do it again. Norman just knew he was going to. For as long as he could remember, every time the family went someplace together, his father drove. And for as long as he could remember, every time they hit a pothole or rough spot on the road, his father would cheerfully say, "Bumpity-bump-bump-bump!"

His mother would grin sweetly, acting as if she'd never heard it before. Little Caleb would repeat the words while Franky and Jessie giggled. The whole Tuttle family loved bumps. The whole family except Norman, that is. He hadn't thought it was funny in a long time, and he certainly wouldn't think it was funny today.

He looked at the cheek on his father's rough face for any sign of movement. They were coming to the crossroads where the snowplows always tore up the intersection. He saw his dad take in a breath and hold it for a moment. Norman gritted his teeth as he heard first the *blunk* of radials over potholes, then the inevitable "Bumpity-bump-bump-bump!" from the front seat.

Norman saw his mother's head in front of him bob along in pleasant agreement.

"Bump-bump," sang Caleb.

Franky and Jessie giggled beside him while they busied themselves with the dismemberment of a Barbie doll.

"Big deal," Norman said, and laid his head against the window, gazing out at the roadside. He thought of the long day of oxymoronic family fun that lay ahead at Winter Carnival, and wished he was going anywhere in the world but there. The dumb parade. The dumb ice skating party. And the dreaded Winter Carnival Dance that night. Norman groaned out loud at the whole sorry shape of it all.

His father frowned into the rearview mirror at Norman's bad attitude, and while he wasn't watching the road, they hit another large pothole. One that bounced them hard enough to whack Norman's head against the door frame. He grabbed his cheekbone and looked sharply at his dad in the mirror.

With no cheer in his voice, and looking Norman square in the eye, his dad said, "Bumpity-bump-bump-bump."

So far it had been a bad year for Norman. Ever since the baby-sitting fiasco at the Flannigans' a month earlier, his life had taken on all the luster of a prison work-release program. He'd been grounded for two months by his parents and forbidden to call by hers. "Maybe we need some space for a while" was about the last thing Laura had said to him. Whatever that meant.

He was allowed to go to school and do chores around the house and on the boat—period. Laura avoided him at school. Comfort evaded him at home. He scraped ice from the porch steps. Chopped wood. Carried wood. Shoveled snow. Norman's days were, to his way of thinking, a collage of toil and confinement. When he could stand it no longer and tried to call Laura, her mother would coldly say that she was "not available."

Under these restrictions Norman was becoming not only heartsick but dangerously overexposed to his own family. The little kids, he decided, were born and bred solely for the purpose of tormenting their oldest brother into nervous conniptions. He'd find plastic spiders under his pillow and dried moose turds in his underwear drawer.

"Stay out of my room!" he'd scream. He'd complain to his mother, who didn't seem to care.

"They're just having some fun with you, dear," she counseled. "Go along with it."

One night his parents went out to some fisheries meeting.

Norman was left in charge and, out of utter revenge, told Franky he had to stay in his room.

"Help! Help!" Franky yelled out of the upstairs window. "I'm being held prisoner by a dork!"

Norman ignored it and continued to watch TV in the living room below. Franky had the bright idea to hang and drop from his bedroom, past the living room window, and land in the snowbank below. He caught Norman's attention with a spine-chilling scream as he flashed past the window on the way down.

Pretending to have fallen while trying to escape, Franky writhed in pain in the snow outside. The thought that he was actually hurt was enough to lure Norman out onto the porch for a look at his brother's pitiful performance.

"Next time try to land on your head, okay?" was all he said before returning to the couch.

Things with his dad were no better. The evening kitchen-table cribbage games had disintegrated into a few after-dinner directives.

"Did you get that wood stacked?"

"Yes."

"Do your homework?"

"Right now."

Norman would retreat to his room for longer and longer stretches. He'd listen to the biting winter winds nosing around his window frame and make lists in his head of every-thing he hated about his life.

His brothers and sister wouldn't leave him alone.

His teachers wouldn't leave him alone. "You missed three homework assignments," they'd whine. "You've dropped a whole grade in history."

His mom wouldn't leave him alone. "Are you getting enough to eat, sweetie? Do you feel okay?"

His dad wouldn't leave him alone. "I ran into Mr. Bietter today. He tells me you're falling behind in his class. What's goin' on, bub?"

I'm stuck inside this life with you. That's what's goin' on, he thought.

"His tests aren't fair," he said.

With the car finally parked at the frozen lake in the center of town, Norman wouldn't even get out for the parade. He didn't see much sense in standing out in the cold just to watch a fire truck and a police car go by. The outhouse races used to make him laugh until he cried. But that seemed long ago and in another life.

Today it was embarrassing to witness. To see his mom and dad laughing and pointing, calling out to the contestants, who rode their contraptions in silly costumes, grinning and waving like they were really somebody doing something. It was all so dumb, Norman thought, and he sank lower into the backseat and slid further inside the collar of his parka and climbed deeper into the gloom.

He barely fit into the parka. Norman's growth in the past two years had been awesome. "You can stand him still and watch him grow out of his clothes," his dad would joke to his mother. It was almost true.

The rubber boots he'd worn at the beginning of the summer were a squeeze by the end. Last year's rain gear hit well above his wrists. The sport coat he'd worn to eighth-grade graduation was already closer to Franky's size than his own.

His legs would ache through the night with the pain of rapid growth. Sometimes his rib cage would seem to seize in a cardiac moment. When his breath returned, he would feel bigger. And on top of these very real growing pains, Norman had the equal discomfort of not knowing exactly how large he'd become at any given moment. He was forever pounding his head on car door frames. His knees would knock the table as he sat down, spilling two of the milks. He missed stairs and stumbled, turned too soon into rooms and barked his cheek on corners. He looked like a marionette when he ran, so he didn't. He walked, ambled, shuffled from place to place.

His voice had changed and was now splattered with bursts of high-pitched croaking, usually while making a shrill point about some injustice. His face had broken out, and the main motivating factor in his life had gone from his bicycle to the telephone, which he was no longer allowed to use.

With all this going on, it wasn't surprising that Norman would begin to see the world as an increasingly hostile place to live. Everything and everybody had changed. It was like waking up in a different body that nobody recognized.

"It's me—Norman," he wanted to say, but he wasn't so convinced himself these days.

As the windows frosted over and the heat left the car, he reluctantly pulled on a pair of his dad's old skates and emerged to join the skaters on the lake.

"Norman. Hey! Stormin' Norman!" Stanley Bindel, arms flailing, speed-skated toward him on the lake, and Norman could see that he was attempting to raise his hand for a flyby high five. Norman hated slapping five. It was stupid. It looked good when athletes on television did it, but they really did it. Fives had to be robust or they were worthless.

Norman, on the spot, held his hand up, and Stanley brushed it awkwardly with his own a split second before he slipped, gyrated, and landed on his backside.

"Grow up, Stanley," Norman said, looking away, refusing to be entertained by his friend's dramatics.

Stanley made convincing gagging noises, and when Norman finally did look at him, he deadpanned, "Oh, I thought you said 'throw up.' My mistake."

Norman looked embarrassed to be there. Many things separate the men from the boys, as they say, but none so literally or so effectively as biology, and Norman easily grouped himself with the men. He and Stanley were only a few months apart in age, but nature's way with boys had, for the time being, put Norman light-years ahead of his friend. There is nothing in this world more destructive to friendship and loyalty than a badly timed hormone or two.

Stanley pulled himself up and staggered to get back on top of his skates. There was hurt on his face, and it wasn't coming from his butt. Norman couldn't conceal the aversion he felt toward his old friend. Luckily he didn't have to for long. Over Stanley's shoulder he spotted Laura Magruder by the warming shack, and the sight of her stopped his breathing.

"What is it, Norm?" Stanley clowned at Norman's stricken look with a new meanness in his voice. "A death in the family? Indigestion?" He turned with mock surprise. "No, it's Laura, queen of the Norman."

"*Grow up,* Stanley!" Norman pushed past his friend, who was again gagging on cue.

As Norman skated across to the warming shack, Laura looked up and spotted him coming. He sent her a meaningful smile, glad to see her for the first time away from school in weeks. But what Laura did in return was unsettling. She looked at him but pretended not to see him. She quickly turned to her girlfriends and, as one, they shimmied out into the mass of townspeople rotating around the lake. Norman coasted to a stop and stood bewildered, rocking on his skate blades.

"Whatcha do, lose your girlfriend?" Laura's older brother, Burt, sat on the hood of his pickup with three of his friends. They all sent Norman those peculiar sadistic sneers that only rabid wolverines and seniors in high school can manage. The force of it drove Norman into the throng of skaters.

He'd gone in to hide but then looked up and found he'd skated right up beside Laura, who was just as surprised.

"Norman, oh, hi!" she said, and pretended to have to focus precisely on her feet.

The chill from Laura was colder than the wind off the lake, but Norman found the words. "Are you going to the dance tonight?"

Laura continued her precision skating. "It's Winter Carnival. *Everybody's* going to be there," she said, and Norman knew then for sure that she wasn't going to be there with him.

The strength seemed to go from his legs. All the things he meant to say roared in his head: I'm sorry. I miss you. Don't leave me. But "Maybe I'll see you" was all he could manage before letting himself drift to a stop outside the skaters. He leaned up against a stack of old tires from the ice derby and surveyed the newly minted miserable world.

Norman saw Laura, skating easily now, talking earnestly with her girlfriends, who stole knowing glances in his direction. His heart felt like it had popped and now hung in tatters on his ribs. Stanley Bindel darted by and Norman had to look away. One of Stanley's goofy looks or stupid remarks right now might lead to felony charges if Norman caught up with him.

He saw Burt and his buddies over on their pickups nodding to their music and sipping at brown bags. Burt looked over again and narrowed his eyes with some ill-defined threat. To avoid it, Norman turned his attention back to the warming shack.

Franky, Jessie, and Caleb were spilling hot chocolate all over themselves, laughing at their mom and dad hamming it up out on the ice. Norman's parents were both graceful skaters and floated across the ice backward and forward, arm in arm, smiling and enjoying themselves. His dad would pretend to lose his balance, flap his arms, and wobble his knees for the benefit of his small audience.

It would have been very funny, Norman thought, if it

wasn't so stupid. If everything wasn't so stupid. And he stalked to the car to wait until the whole stupid thing was over with.

Norman was even quieter on the way home. His dad eyed him from time to time in the rearview mirror.

"You okay, Norm?"

"Perfect," Norman grumbled.

Norman had his head against the window again, and all he could do was swirl the misery around his mind like the skaters on the lake. Laura and Stanley and mean seniors and demented siblings, and . . . *bam!* The window frame came up and cracked him right in the chin.

"Bumpity-bump-bump-bump" came his father's voice cheerfully from the front seat. His mom grinned wearily.

"Bump-bump," went Caleb.

Franky and Jessie laughed. And Norman lost his better judgment.

"Would you please stop saying that stupid thing every time we hit a bump! You say it *every time*, and it drives me crazy! So would you please stop it!"

Silence hung in the car like a frozen corpse. His mother's neck muscles tensed. The three littler ones sensed danger and shrank together in a wad of snow pants. Norman heard his tone of voice still fresh in his ears, and his blood flowed backward. Had he really said that to his father? There were going to be consequences for this. But what?

His dad continued to drive but spent most of his time looking in the mirror at Norman. He was taking those long, deep breaths like he did on the boat before he was going to pull on something really hard. And then he spoke in a tone so cool and flat it made Norman tremble.

"There's only two people in this world I'll let talk to me like that, and you aren't one of them. What in blazes has come over you lately?"

Norman looked at his dad's face, and the anger and the sadness and the fear of what was happening to him gushed out of Norman's eyes and out of his mouth in one damp flow.

"Laura is breaking up with me, Stanley Bindel's a total loser, and everybody hates me! Including you!"

Another silence filled the car, a little warmer than the last. The man in the front seat studied the road for a long mile, then studied in the mirror the boy sunk down in his parka like he'd just plain die there.

The soreness and sorrow of fourteen-going-on-fifteen clung to Norman as plain as skate blisters. He didn't need a lecture. He didn't need disciplining. It wasn't a time for speeches. It was time for inspiration, and the father appeared to search deep inside for the words.

He wasn't watching the road very well, and the car hammered in and out of a series of potholes like gunfire. Words sprang to his lips, but then he met Norman's eyes in the mirror and saw a sad young man who didn't need any more punishment right now.

"Rough road," he allowed. "Isn't it, Norm?"

Norman looked back at his dad but couldn't answer. His mother's neck muscles relaxed. The Three Creepies eased apart and breathed again. And Norman silently agreed with his father for the first time in many weeks.

PARTIES UNKNOWN

The party hadn't really been his fault. It just sort of happened to him—like everything else these days. After all, it was his parents' dumb idea to take the kids over to Valdez to visit with Grandma and Grandpa Tuttle. Norman had begged and stomped and pleaded and pouted not to go. "It's so *boring* at their house. They don't *do* anything."

Norman knew that spring avalanches regularly clogged the roads between here and Anchorage for hours, even days. "It could take two days just to get there! And we could get stuck up there! What about school?"

His dad scoffed. "Like you've been concerned with that lately. Listen, son, your Grandpa Tuttle's old and not so well. There may not be a whole lot of opportunities left to see him." Norman's father had let the implication dangle, but Norman neglected to reach for it.

"But I've got a date with Laura on Saturday night to the April Fool's Dance. It's our first date since . . . since . . ." Since I got her busted over at the Flannigans', he thought. Norman searched for the words everywhere but in his father's eyes. "Dad, I *have* to go."

The older Tuttle shook his head sadly and dismissed his son. "If it's a fool's dance, then I guess you'd better be there."

The family left on Saturday morning. His father's silence rang in the empty house long after the car had disappeared down the road. His mother had left a kiss on his forehead and a three-page note on the refrigerator.

There are hot dogs and beans in the blue Tupperware. Pot pies are in the basement freezer. Don't forget to turn off the oven. Feed the cats. Lock the doors. DO YOUR HOMEWORK. No shoes in the house. Stay out of your dad's candy bars. . . .

Norman flipped ahead through an endless list of chores and kitchen safety tips until on the last page a message in bold block letters commanded his attention: *ABSOLUTELY NO FRIENDS IN THE HOUSE.* It closed with *We'll be home on Tuesday if the roads stay open. Love, Mom.*

Norman put the pages back up with a banana magnet and talked to himself. " 'Do this. Don't do that. No-no, Norman.' They think I have to be told everything like a little kid!"

Norman rummaged around in the top cupboard for one of his dad's chocolate bars. Then, as he wandered into the living room for some spiritual communing with his PlayStation, he let his mind drift to where it usually did if left unattended: Laura Magruder. Soft, sweet-smelling Laura Magruder, who had returned once again to his life. He'd almost gotten used to her being out of reach when one day that week she'd popped out of a crowd of juniors and seniors and sidled up to him in the hall.

"Going to the dance Saturday?"

Norman looked past her to the group of upperclassmen. "Is this an April Fool's joke?" he asked.

Laura stroked his arm with the backs of two fingers. "You're so funny."

"Yeah," he gulped. "I'll be there."

With that memory, and with most of Norman's thinking being done far south of his brain these days, it was possible for his thoughts to linger somewhere between Laura's magic touch and the acrylic grip of a video game. That's where he stayed through most of the afternoon, emerging only long enough to shower, change, and walk out to the road to meet Burt, Jackie, and Laura for his ride to the dance.

"So your parents are gone for the weekend?" Laura said after their first dance.

"Uh, yeah." Norman didn't trust the look on Laura's face, but it turned him completely to goo all the same. "The whole tribe went."

"I've never been to your house before." Laura ran her hand up the side of Norman's leg, and suddenly the temperature in the high school all-purpose room rose seventeen hundred degrees—to approximately the temperature of hell. A personal hell that would last well into Norman's next morning.

A fish burp in a riptide has more control over its destiny than Norman Tuttle did in the presence of Laura Magruder. Her push-tug affections had stripped him of all sense of dignity, and anything he knew for sure was lost in a fog of desire. Any suggestion that came out of Laura's mouth seemed ultimately doable. More than doable, actually; it became mandatory. And always there was her unspoken promise of something. Something undefined. Laura ran her finger around Norman's shirt collar. *That.*

"You can't tell anybody!" Norman whispered urgently to Laura.

"We have to tell Burt and Jackie. They're our ride."

Norman was freaked but spineless. "Okay, but *they* can't tell anybody either."

"Don't worry," Laura said as she made her way into the throng of dancers to find her brother. It was the last encouraging thing Norman would hear that night.

The foursome looked out Norman's front window uneasily. Laura was the first to speak. "I didn't tell anybody."

"I didn't tell anybody," Jackie said next, "unless you count Jessica, but you can't mean her because she's my best friend and she graduated last year too and she wouldn't tell anybody either, except maybe her little sister who might have told Jason, but they're going steady now so it's not like a big deal or anything."

"I hope your dad paid his insurance" was all Burt had to offer as he settled into the cushions of Norman's father's favorite chair and stretched as if to go to sleep.

Norman could not summon a molecule of serenity from anywhere in his being. He paced in front of the window watching the line of headlights making their way up the barren country road.

"This can't happen. You've got to make them go away, Burt. Laura?" His voice was so pitiful-sounding it almost squeaked. Nobody looked at him.

The cars made their way first past the Flannigans' dark and empty house. Then they were passing the Bindels'. Stay home, Stanley. Just stay home.

In Norman's dilated eyes the headlights all became one moving mass of swirling light. An inferno. Out of control. Unpredictable. The party took off like flame in the wind with only Norman to fight the fire.

"You can't stay. Take your muddy shoes off! No, don't take your shoes off, just leave. You can't stay!" Norman started his impotent refrain while the happy herd poured in the door. "You can't stay. We're not allowed. My parents will kill me and send you the head.

"That's my parents' bedroom. Don't go in there. Don't touch that. Those are my dad's candy bars. You can't stay, you can't stay, you can't stay, you *can't stay!*"

Stanley Bindel came in the door wearing his heavy coat over striped pajamas. The kids in the kitchen howled with approval. "Great party, Norm," Stanley said. "Too bad your parents are going to send you to Afghanistan when they find out about it. Where's the soda?"

"Go home, Stanley," Norman said, and kept moving.

For the first time in a year Norman forgot all about Laura. She was submerged somewhere in the throng that was continuing to move through the house like gremlins, picking things up, moving furniture, laughing at family portraits. Somebody put techno dance music on his parents' big, dumb console stereo and turned it up so loud that it sounded like the woofers were about to spit up blood.

Burt's buddies showed up with beer. They disappeared into the living room with several other seniors Norman didn't even know by name.

Norman went through the house on a mad search for Laura. He needed her help to plead with Burt to get the beer out of the house. It took him a good half hour, between clearing a couple out of his parents' bedroom, breaking up a fight over the PlayStation, and hiding the whipped cream from the wrestling squad. Finally he found her in the living room with her brother's gang, sitting on the lap of a senior who was flipping his cigarette ash into Mrs. Tuttle's jade plant.

She looked at him with poorly disguised triumph on her face. "What's the matter, Norman? Never seen a party before? Maybe if you brought out some *pizza*, everything would get better."

A shock wave passed through Norman. Laura had done this to him. On purpose. But there was no time even for a broken heart.

Alcohol. Cigarettes. He could be grounded until he reached retirement age. Even banishment to the caves of Afghanistan would not satisfy them on this one. This would mean his eternal soul. There was only one thing left to do.

"I'm calling the cops," he said on the way to the kitchen phone, noticing yet another car pulling up to the house.

"What'd he say?" said Burt after him.

"He said he was calling the cops." The senior holding Laura looked at her and asked, "Is he bluffing?"

Laura bit her lip. "I can't tell, but we might want to get out of here all the same."

"Cops!" The alarm went up.

"Cops!" somebody repeated upstairs.

Norman ignored the commotion and marched to the phone on the wall. Everyone was at the kitchen door trying to get out all at once. Being most familiar with the terrain, Stanley Bindel led the pack and struggled to pull the door open against the press of bodies behind him. When the door finally cleared, everyone froze. It was Stanley's voice that cut through the sound of breath being sucked into two dozen sets of teenage lungs at once.

"Mr. Tuttle! What are *you* doing home?"

Norman almost swallowed the phone receiver.

"Nine-one-one emergency. What is the nature of your emergency?"

The sea of heads parted between Norman and his father. The look on his dad's face was somewhere between tears and homicide. Norman felt his eternal soul burning through the bottoms of his shoes.

"What is the nature of your emergency?"

Norman looked at his father. He found Laura's mortified face. He saw Burt palming a beer and heading for the front door.

"Wrong number, operator," he said absently, and dropped the phone. "Totally wrong."

It had taken until nearly three o'clock in the morning to clean up the worst offenses. Norman's brothers and sister walked through the house, wide-eyed and reverent. It was a train wreck of a screw-up. This was the biggest trouble they'd ever seen.

"Norman," Jessie whispered to herself, as if speaking of the dead.

Franky could scarcely conceal his delight. "Yer gonna fry, big brother. Fry like fish."

Caleb sucked his thumb for the first time in a year and examined candy bar wrappers for leavings.

Norman's mother hustled them to bed without a word and disappeared into her own room. Ashen-faced, she emerged briefly a few minutes later to drop an empty beer can into the garbage.

Later, as he worked his way down the hall with a bucket and sponge, Norman thought he heard her crying through the closed door. Maybe it was crying. He'd never heard her cry before. But it sure wasn't laughing. He could have stuck his head in the bucket and drowned.

He cursed the avalanche in the pass near Anchorage that had closed the road and turned them back. He cursed his parents for not calling ahead. He cursed himself for being so stupid.

His father's silence was making him crazy. No yelling. No stomping around. He just sat at the kitchen table giving short, quiet directions. "Vacuum the living room. Straighten the books. Get whatever that is off the wall." Between these instructions an icy quiet hung around Norman's dad like a force field.

Stunned and deliberate, Norman went about his duties. What was it going to be? Military academy? The Foreign Legion? Obedience school? Maybe they'd make him live in a damp hole out back. They'd drop small bits of food through a metal grille. That would be okay. Anything would be better than this silent treatment. It made Norman want to bolt for the door.

Run away, he thought. That's what he could do! He could sneak away and go to Anchorage. Get a job bagging groceries until he had enough money to fly to Seattle, then work his way down the coast to Mexico, where he could learn to speak Spanish, marry a señorita, have children, grow old, and die, and then it would all be over with.

Norman fancied himself in a sombrero, and it was late enough that it was starting to look good on him. He was just getting into the wife-and-kids part when his dad finally interrupted.

"Norman, you can get the rest tomorrow. Sit down here a minute."

His father's voice did not sound angry, but neither was it kind. Norman sat in the chair across the table and waited. There could be no quieter place in the world at three o'clock in the morning than around this kitchen table after this unbelievably awful night. Norman could hear the lightbulb filament ringing above their heads.

Eventually his dad began. "Norman, I want to tell you a story about my brother."

"Uncle Stu?" Norman said, instantly relieved they weren't talking about him.

"No, my older brother. He'd be your uncle Oliver. That is, if he's still alive. Nobody's heard from him in over thirty years."

Norman was perplexed. "I thought it was just you and Uncle Stu."

"That's what Dad—Grandpa Tuttle—wanted everybody to think, and that's why I need to tell you about Oliver tonight. It can't wait another day."

It never occurred to Norman to question what was being said. He could only rest his head on his hands and listen with an expression of intensity mirroring his father's.

"Oliver was my big brother. Great guy. Took me hunting, taught me how to fish, mend net, pilot a boat. Stu was a little younger. I taught him, but Dad taught Oliver. They were close. Dad was always telling him what a fine fisherman he made. Oliver was allowed to take the family boat out for trips on his own by the time he was your age. Dad had big plans for Oliver.

"But as good a fisherman as Oliver was, he had a lot of mischief in him. Just normal stuff for a boy that age—girls, pranks, a little drinking—but you know how tightly wound your grandpa is about those kinds of things. And Oliver had a knack for letting it get out of hand. He was such a nice fella that he'd let his friends talk him into anything.

"One time they all got caught joyriding in Fritz Ferguson's truck. When the police brought Oliver up to the house, Dad went berserk. He took out his Bible and beat Oliver with it until he cried—until Dad cried, that is. Oliver just stood and took it. Didn't say a thing. He had bruises on him for weeks after. He'd look at them every night in our room before he went to sleep. He'd just sit in the lamplight touching those Bible bruises with his fingers and not say a word.

"I don't remember Oliver and Dad ever talking to each other again. Except one night. Oliver was about eighteen or so, I guess, and he'd been living on the boat for a while. I didn't know what he did with his time. He'd stopped paying attention to me along with everybody else. Well then, one night Oliver shows up at the door all sheepish and shuffling. The rest of us got scooted out of earshot while he and Dad sat down.

"Next thing we knew all glory broke loose out in the kitchen. Dad was just about choking on his tongue, he was so mad. He was cussing a blue streak in between chapter and verse and poor Mom didn't know whether to cover our ears or fall down and pray. Oliver finally blasted through the door and ran outside just ahead of Dad's Bible. We found it later layin' a good forty feet from the house. Dad had flung it right at him but missed. Good thing—it might have killed him."

Norman's dad took a breath. "He might as well have killed him. It was the last time we ever saw our brother. And Dad never spoke of him again.

"Of course, as small as this town is, we didn't have too much trouble figuring out what had gone on. It seems Oliver had gotten a girl pregnant. Nobody even knew they were seeing each other, but that's because she was only sixteen and they were sneaky. Oliver was in a lot of trouble, but he loved the girl, and he'd come to ask Dad for help. The times being what they were, he had no other place to turn.

"Well, Oliver and this girl disappeared. It was a terrible scandal at church and all, and Dad moved us over to Valdez so he didn't have to face people. He still doesn't like coming back here, as you know. The girl's family moved out too, and as far as this town is concerned, those two kids never existed. Me and Stu were forbidden to ever mention our brother again. Mom must have been keeping some promise to Dad, because she wouldn't allow it either. He was just gone."

Norman stared at his father's whiskers, trying to take it all in. He might as well have just been told that he was adopted. The family he thought he belonged to wasn't really his. This new family was his. What a weird thing to keep a secret, he thought. He could hardly believe, after all these years, that the never-make-waves and never-a-discouraging-word Tuttle family history actually had some action in it. It explained something. Or was trying to.

He chewed the insides of his cheeks as if digesting the new information. His dad rubbed his face and looked directly into Norman's eyes.

"Dad's gonna leave this world without knowing if his oldest boy is alive or dead. Oliver and your granddad forgot how to talk to each other. Just like a switch was thrown, it was over between them. That's why you don't have an uncle Oliver."

Norman's father got up from his chair and stood over him. "When you fell off the boat that day, I swore that kind of thing would never happen to us. And we're a long way from it . . . I hope. It appears I don't make all the decisions in the matter." He put a hand on Norman's shoulder. "Do I?"

"Guess not," Norman allowed.

"Your schoolwork is falling off. Stanley doesn't come around . . ." He stopped there, remembering his homecoming. "Not like he used to. The Magruders don't want you around their daughter. I don't understand, Norm. It's like you're determined to push everything worthwhile out of your life."

Norman stood up and let his dad hold him by the shoulders. From the back of his head a voice cried, I don't understand either, Dad. I'm not a bad person. Am I? Am I, Dad?

But the voice up front could not speak. Norman just flushed and shrugged and let his father finish.

"You go up to bed now and think about what we're going to do about this trouble tonight. We'll talk about it in the morning."

Norman Tuttle sat at his bedroom window watching the darkness dwindle. It went in fits and starts. The same way the snow melts this time of year in this part of Alaska. It begins with dirty patches of gray, wet grass pushing up through the seasoned snow. Ever so gradually it becomes dirty patches of snow left scattered on the gray grass. And finally it is all gray grass, lifelessly waiting for the sun.

Norman's head was filled with the buzzing mush that comes of a night without rest. Well beyond the urge for sleep, he could only stare at the world as it slowly brightened and the vague dark shapes in the twilight took form, assembling themselves into another day. When the sun finally did show itself, Norman found a world wholly unchanged from the day before, yet different in every way.

He looked around the room. There was the piggy bank he'd had since he could remember, now with a Megadeth decal on its pink flanks. A poster of military aircraft hung next to a needlepoint sampler of the Twenty-third Psalm his mother had placed there five years ago. *Even though I walk through the valley of the shadow . . .*

A plastic bat and ball stood in one corner. His deer rifle hung crookedly on two nails. Boxer shorts and one sock dangled from the forked antlers screwed to the door. *I will fear no evil . . .* This was his sanctuary. This was his soul.

Norman picked up the framed picture of him and Laura from the sill and sat watching the morning come. The sun behind the mountains across the bay brought a relief of color into the world, but it cast little light on Norman's gray mood. Everywhere he looked he saw his life, and it looked exactly like dirty snow and dead grass. He looked at the photo.

She set me up, he brooded. No. Her brother set me up. But she went along with it. Or maybe he went along with her. Either way, they screwed me.

As if to clear it all from his mind, the dawn continued to brighten. Norman set the photo down again and it soon became impossible for him to hold his attention within the confines of his room, or even the dismal yard.

The sun, still behind the mountains, glowed atomic red

like the light in a bad wilderness painting at a mall art store. Too bright to be real. Too vast to be believed. Finally he let his reluctant gaze travel across to the glimmering bay and mountain vista. It was a view he looked at every day but rarely noticed anymore. *He leads me beside still waters . . .* Today it was transporting.

Somewhere beyond these dark valleys and across these still waters was an uncle he'd never met. And however far Oliver had gone, and whether or not he lived and breathed, he was for the moment the closest person to Norman in the whole family.

"So," he said to the rising sun. "I'm not the original screw-up after all."

Norman pictured his grandpa and the Bible and the beating. "I guess my dad could be worse."

Amber sunlight filled his room, and Norman warmed to the thought. It could be worse. A tired smile tugged at his face. Then he heard water run. The stairs creaked, and a cupboard door closed down in the kitchen. The sun slipped free of the mountain shadows and the soft amber light turned to clear white. The night was over.

Norman's smile evaporated. There was much more to talk about with the man downstairs, and things soon would get worse. If he was sure of nothing else, he was sure of that.

POINTS SOUTH

"Would you like some more peas, Norman?" Emily Flannigan held a steaming bowl with both hands. She smiled, her eyebrows raised.

Norman looked at her from across the table and thought it over. It was a fair question. Straightforward. To the point. That's why he couldn't think of an answer right off the bat.

Back home with his family he would have had all kinds of possibilities to sort through with a simple question like that. His mother might have said, *Would you like some more peas, Norman?* but she'd have meant, *You should eat some more peas, they're good for you.*

His dad would have sat at the other end of the table, saying nothing but meaning, *Your mother worked hard on this meal. You should show some appreciation.* The Creepies would sit quietly, concentrating on their own food, thinking, *How come Norman gets so many peas?*

Norman's knee bounced wildly under the table. He glanced anxiously around the kitchen before hazarding his reply. "Um—no, I don't think so, Mrs. Flannigan. I'm full?"

"Okay. And please call me Emily." She set the bowl down again and went back to her own meal. Ed Flannigan looked out the window, chewing absently. The three younger Flannigans passively ate their dinners, oblivious to the exchange.

Norman felt the strain ease out of his frame. He stabbed another piece of pot roast on his plate and breathed again. Being away from his family was going to take some getting used to.

He ate with no pleasure and retraced the steps that brought him to this strange table with these displaced neighbors over a thousand miles south of everything he knew for sure.

Some things happen by design. Some things happen by accident. And some things just happen. Norman's dry mouth worked the meat into a flavorless paste while he wondered why it had all happened to him. The last six weeks had spun completely out of control.

Ever since the party Norman's world had been a hostile environment. At first his mom and dad had been pretty calm about finding two dozen of Norman's friends and schoolmates drinking, smoking, and carrying on in their house, but that had only been shock. By the following morning they had regained control of their faculties and were acting more like themselves—intolerable.

First off, they had grounded him indefinitely, or "until the cows come home," as his father put it. The Tuttles did not own livestock.

Norman hadn't helped his case any by sneaking out of the house one Friday night to try to see Laura at the bowling alley. His dad had found him within an hour.

"What were you trying to prove?"

Norman's mind raced. I had to see Laura. She won't talk to me at school. She won't answer my calls. I'm losing my mind over this. But all Norman said was, "I dunno."

"Are you losing your mind?"

"No!"

Every day after school Norman was given another endless and grisly chore to perform around the house, and by far the grisliest and most interminable chore of all was cleaning up the yard.

Springtime in Alaska resembles less a changing of the seasons than it does the unearthing of a forgotten landfill. With winter comprising a generous portion of an Alaska year, fully half of everything that hits the ground in Alaska hits it in the wintertime and reveals itself all at once in the spring when the snows recede.

Norman had stood out in his parents' yard picking trash, sticks, toys, and tools out of the mud. There was the end of a broken snow shovel. A wet and decaying rolled newspaper.

A metal toy dump truck that had been mangled by the snow-blower. A petrified mitten. He could feel the still-thawing ground squeeze and give under his feet.

Norman sighed at the pointlessness of it all. The greening of the landscape did nothing to recover his spirits. There are only a few things that grow in Alaska in the early spring, all worthless, mostly weeds. He'd seen it all before.

The budding alder, sprouting dandelions, greening willow, and semi-comatose grasses were all lost on Norman. As he looked around the flat bench of acreage from which their parcel of land was carved, then beyond to the greater bay panorama ringed by mountains, his thoughts were narrow and bleak. Everything before him could be described with one of three words: *trees*, *weeds*, or *rocks*.

Looking back toward his corner of the world, Norman noticed his father watching him from the kitchen window, which only annoyed him. He mocked his father: "Can't you work any faster than that? You missed a stick. Let's at least get it to look like somebody lives here. Sometime today, okay, Norman?"

Norman bent over for a stick and looked at his father through his legs. "Hey, Dad, look, it's a full moon!"

Norman was laughing at his own cleverness when his dad started motioning through the window for him to come in the house. His nerves surged for just a moment before realizing his father couldn't possibly have heard him. He dropped everything where he stood and headed for the back door still talking to himself.

"It's heart-to-heart time, boys and girls. What's it going to be today? The 'I almost lost you once by not paying attention. Now I feel like I'm losing you because I *am* paying attention' heartbreaker? How about the 'If you want us to trust you again, you'll have to earn it' rant?"

Once or twice a week his dad would call him to the kitchen before the rest of the family had gathered for dinner, and they'd *talk*. Sometimes his mom would sit with them, not saying much, sometimes reaching to stroke Norman's hair before he dodged the hand and sent eye daggers her way. Or she would be at the sink, listening and delivering meaningful looks at strategic moments. The Creepies would wander in and out, oblivious except for Franky, who took great pleasure in his older brother's troubles and tried to eavesdrop from the doorway until chased away.

But mostly it would be just Norman and his dad.

He used to love that. Having his dad to himself. He'd once craved it. Now it seemed excruciating. His dad's "I almost lost you" was getting repetitious and tired.

I fell off your boat. You came back and got me. Get over it.

The talks usually amounted to the recitation of one of the aforementioned lectures while Norman picked at his face and studied the pattern in the Formica. The message to his parents was clear: Keep me home, treat me like a kid, work me like a slave—you will pay.

Norman dropped his coat and kicked off his muddy boots inside the kitchen door. He walked over to the table without looking up and took a seat. His mom was nowhere in sight. His dad was at the counter. "Kind of damp out there this afternoon. Cup of coffee, Normy?"

Normy? Norman looked at his dad skeptically but welcomed the coffee. It smelled of better days. Norman relaxed a little with the hot mug, thinking that things couldn't possibly get any weirder than they already were. But he'd been wrong about a lot of things lately.

His dad sat down looking sad, even guilty. Norman's stomach knotted. "Norm," he began, "your mother and I have had a couple of real nice chats with the Flannigans this week. They're getting settled down in Oregon, you know."

Norman could hardly hear his dad over all the warning bells going off in his head. This was coming out of nowhere. What did the Flannigans have to do with anything? Norman's knees were jiggling at about ten kilohertz under the table as his father went on.

"Well, it seems they've moved onto an old farm, and Ed has taken it upon himself to get it going. Ed says there's no work around there, and he might as well do something useful with his time while Emily teaches at that college. So as it turns out, he's getting kind of a late start on the year and could use some good help."

Norman, numb and waiting, was staring at one of the hairs coming out of his father's nose.

"Your mother and I talked about it and decided there was nothing for you around here this summer but more trouble. Me and your uncle Stu can handle the boat without you this year. So, what do you think of sunny Oregon for a while?" With false good cheer Norman's father took a long sip of his coffee and looked at his son through the steam.

Norman could think of nothing to say. It was as if someone had come bounding up and said, *We're going to shoot you in the morning. What do you think?*

Norman wasn't thinking. He was just sitting there bouncing his knees and staring at his dad's nostrils and letting everything drain away. Every last vestige of control over his own life melted down out of him and left one singular concern emblazoned across his face: Laura Magruder. Broken heart. Now banishment. Why didn't they just shoot him?

His father read him perfectly.

"Let go of it, Norman. The Magruders have asked twice that you stop calling over there. This place is nothing but trouble for you right now. I mean, we were doing so *good*, you and me. Then there's fights . . ."

Fights? I was afraid! Norman thought, remembering big Leonard Kopinski. "It wasn't a fight! And that was last year!" he cried.

His dad ignored him and continued, "That mess at the Flannigans' . . ."

Okay, that was a stupid thing to do. "They weren't supposed to come home!"

"That harebrained party of yours . . ."

Laura did that. To me! She did it *to* me! "It wasn't my party!"

"Violating your grounding and sneaking out . . ."

"Once!" Norman objected, but he was thinking, She won't talk to me! She's seeing a senior! I have to know why!

"A little time away will be good for you. For us. Maybe it will get your head screwed back on straight. You haven't thought past your next date with that girl in a year. There's a whole great big world out there, Norman, and you're getting stuck in a little one of your own invention. You'll leave the day after school is out. Ed's waiting for you down there and he'll pay you fairly."

Norman's exile had begun less than twenty-four hours ago. His dad had driven him to Anchorage for the flight to Portland only this morning. Ed Flannigan had met him at the airport for the long drive to the farm. Four months earlier Emily Flanni-gan had taken a teaching position at a college. Rumor had it that Ed was furious about leaving Alaska. Threatened divorce, even. And here they were.

"If it isn't Al Capone," he said when Norman stepped out of the terminal.

"No," Norman countered quietly as he shook the out-stretched hand, embarrassed to be facing him again. Like this. "Sorry for all the trouble, Mr. Flannigan."

"No trouble for me. I can use the help," he said, tossing Norman's duffel into the trunk. "My Eddie isn't quite big enough to do much but get underfoot. And call me Ed."

"Okay . . . Ed." Norman tried it on.

"So your folks tell me you blew it again." Ed spoke matter-of-factly.

"Sorta."

"Sorta," Ed teased. He steered the car onto the freeway and picked up speed. "Why do you do it, Norman?"

"Do what?"

"Buck your parents like you do."

"I don't."

"You do."

"I don't mean to."

"Ah . . . temporary insanity. That it?" Ed laughed.

"Yeah. Kinda," Norman said, impressed with Ed's accuracy.

Ed laughed again. "Love makes you crazy, Norman. I'll allow you that. Let me guess—that Magruder girl ties you in knots, and there's not a darn thing you can do about it. So you take it out on the people you know how to hurt the most—your folks."

Norman said nothing.

"Am I getting warm?"

Norman stared down the highway.

"You start blowin' off school. Sneakin' around. Listening to the wrong people. Next thing you know you're in it over your head—but you won't admit you're bein' a jerk and made a mistake. So you blame everybody but yourself for the consequences." Ed shoved Norman's shoulder playfully. "Know why?"

"Why?"

"Because you're becoming a man, buckaroo. You're becoming a man." Ed slapped the side of his own head. "It makes you stupid."

They drove through the flat, wide valleys of central Oregon as though passing through a gauntlet. They arrived at the farm just in time for dinner, Norman nearly staggering over the day's long travel ordeal.

He'd never been out of the state of Alaska in his life. He'd never flown on an airplane. He'd never been this far from home. And he'd never heard the truth about himself before.

Now he looked across the table to Ed, who was staring at him with no expression on his face. Then Ed smiled like a buddy does. A sadness Norman couldn't name made a lump in his throat and threatened to gag him. He didn't think throwing up his first dinner at the Flannigans' was the way to start his summer in Oregon—however awful it promised to be in every other way—and he quickly excused himself to the bathroom.

"What's that all about?" Emily said, looking after him.

Ed just shrugged. "Guy stuff," he said, and spooned himself some more peas.

Late that night Norman lay on his back on the Flannigans' hide-a-bed. Tears of helpless rage came from deep inside him and found their way down the sides of his face to his ears. It tickled, and he had to wipe them.

Norman lay in a discontented daze with his mind far to the north. He was oblivious to the sounds of a foreign night going about its business around him. A chorus of bullfrogs gulped in the distance. Crickets creaked in a rhythm of disarray near and far. A breeze scented with the sweet smell of fallen peaches moved the curtains in the window.

Norman's eyelids bounced twice and stuck shut. The unfamiliar night crept up on him. The air, the sounds, the smells—all worked to smooth the creases on his forehead and draw his mind across the miles from Alaska. When all of Norman was finally in this place, his jaw slacked and a deep rush of air poured from him. The next breath he drew came from someplace new as he dreamed about heaps of peas.

The morning came like a good idea—slow, clear, and divine—pushing everything else out of the way. Norman sat up surprised, not able to remember where he was. The light coming through the window was warm and full. Not the clean white light of Alaska, but a light with something else in it. Oh, that's right, he thought. Oregon. Flannigans.

Looking out the window, all that Norman could see was green and unidentifiable. The grass, the trees, and the bushes along the driveway were all polished with the morning dew. Madrone, manzanita, holly, and peach trees glimmered in the rising light with an almost artificial quality. They were nothing he had ever seen before. They looked shiny and exotic.

The house was quiet and he seemed to be the only one awake. The quiet and the light and the view all lent an otherworldly quality to the morning. It was as if Norman had woken up in another star system. He pulled on his clothes and slipped out the back door.

The tall grass rolled and did slow swirls in the barely moving air. A squirrel sat criticizing Norman in a tall stout oak beside the house. A robin hunted worms in the freshly mowed grass between the house and an old barn. Norman saw movement in the barn's long shadow. He was not alone.

Ed pulled his head out of the middle of an old yellow tractor Norman had taken for junk. He noticed Norman standing on the porch and called to him. "Hey, there's my helper. C'mere, Norm, I could use your two good hands."

Norman stepped off the porch, noticing the ground was solid under his feet as he walked out toward the tractor. Ed stood with a screwdriver in one hand and a wrench in the other. "Up with the chickens, eh, buckaroo?"

Norman rolled his eyes but couldn't hold the corners of his mouth down. Ed Flannigan was the only person besides cheesy television show characters he'd ever heard use the word *buckaroo*. He had a big, goofy smile aimed fully at Norman.

"What a pair of farmers we're gonna make! Climb on up in the driver's seat there. I just got new plugs in 'er. She'll either purr like a kitten or burn like a trash fire."

Norman did as he was told, cautious but willing to be a part of Ed's morning. Ed stabbed a grubby finger at the array of controls screwed to or hanging out of the tractor console.

"Choke. Throttle. Starter," he said without explanation, assuming correctly that Norman knew what to do with them. Norman's time on a fishing boat and behind lawn mowers and snowblowers had taught him the ways of machinery.

Ed leaned into the engine to worry something with the screwdriver. "Okay, choke it, give it about half a throttle, and turn it over."

Norman quickly found the choke and throttle, then held his finger to the starter button and looked to Ed. "Now?"

"Fire away, buckaroo."

Norman pressed the button; the engine struggled for several revolutions and then erupted with a bellow of black smoke. Ed stood watching something inside the engine compartment for a bit, then looked up to Norman gamely. "Let's take 'er for a spin."

He jumped up on the axle behind Norman and leaned forward onto the seat and the boy's back. The closeness was easy and good. "You're going to be the official tractor man, Norm. I got too much work to do in the peach orchard. The gear pattern's on top of the stick there, and watch the clutch, it's pretty sticky."

Norman found first gear with a guess and a grind, and tried to ease the clutch out. It grabbed suddenly and jerked the tractor to life, lifting the front end slightly off the ground.

Ed almost fell, and then laughed. "Take us out around the barn, leadfoot. I'll show you the field."

Ed directed Norman out to what looked like four acres of tall grass. There were already swaths torn out and tractor marks crisscrossing it in all directions. An old wagon and piles of junk, rocks, and debris lay along one fence.

"I've already cleaned 'er out mostly," Ed said over Norman's shoulder. "All we gotta do is plow this under and we're in business."

Ed motioned to continue, so Norman grabbed another gear and pointed them out into the sea of grass. He felt the vibration of the engine rattling his hands and coming up through the seat. The stiff old tractor's bones complained and creaked and popped across the rough ground. When they were deep into the field, Ed touched Norman's shoulder. "Hold up once, Norm."

Norman idled the tractor down and put it in neutral. Ed stood tall on the axle and pointed expansively. "We're in the middle of your sweet corn here. All the way back to that fence'll be corn. Over that way's your tomatoes, peppers, lettuce, and peas. I was going to do eggplant too, but I couldn't sell anything I wouldn't eat myself. And over there along that back fence you'll never guess what you have."

Ed waited for Norman to guess. Norman didn't have a clue.

"Watermelons," he said reverently. "Watermelons and cantaloupes. Can you believe it? I tell you, Norm, you can grow just about anything in this country. Back home it seems like it's gotta be one of three things: trees, rocks, or weeds."

Norman looked back at Ed, surprised, and the two men shared one of those flashes of recognition that feels like a compliment.

The mention of Alaska changed something on Norman's face, and Ed suddenly turned serious. "I didn't wanna come down here either, Norm. I didn't have much choice. Neither do you. It's a crummy deal, I know, but let's have some fun with it, okay?"

"Sure . . . Ed."

"I know you're not a bad kid. And I know you think your dad is a horse's hinder . . ."

Norman grinned and Ed continued.

"He's not. You're both good men. Take a break and don't worry so much. I'll try not to make either one of you sorry that you're here. How's eight bucks an hour sound?"

"Good," Norman said. "Really good," wondering how Ed could afford it, then thinking of his dad.

Ed offered a handshake. Norman took it with the wrong hand, his left, and the grip was awkward. Ed held on long enough to make it seem untroubled, and Norman felt a friend forming in his hand. "First let's get this planted. Pull this bucket of junk back over to the barn and we'll see if we can put a plow on."

As Norman steered back toward the barn and house, he saw Mrs. Flannigan come out on the porch. Missy and Corey, still in their pajamas, swung from the porch rail. Mrs. Flannigan waved big, and they both waved back. Norman sat up, aware of his one hand on the wheel and the other on the shift lever. For all its rattling and popping, the tractor moved with sureness through the field. Norman was driving it. Ed stood holding on behind him.

When they got to the barn, Norman switched off the motor and they heard kind scolding from the porch. "As long as you have everybody awake around here on a Saturday morning, you might as well come in and eat something. Norman, do you want some waffles?"

Norman could still feel the tractor resonating in his bones. He jumped down onto the solid ground. "I'd love some waffles, Mrs. Flannigan," he said, not thinking of anything for the first time in a long while. "I'm *really* hungry."

"Good then," she said. "Wipe your feet. And call me Emily."

IN OLIVER'S SHADOW

As the airliner banked south for its final approach, the clouds scattered and the city of Seattle, where Norman would connect with his flight to Alaska, presented itself like a showpiece. The plane had been in clouds all the way from Portland, and the sudden city view was startling. A quiet gasp escaped him and fogged the window, and he wiped it clear again with his sleeve.

Norman could pick out the Space Needle. They passed over the baseball and football stadiums, either of which could hold the entire population of his hometown ten or twenty times over. His eyes tracked the endless grid of streets and highways teeming with the midday traffic. Whoever they were and wherever they were going, he was certain it was a thousand times more interesting than his destination.

Norman was going home. His family was waiting for him. The school grind and small-town Alaska were there to pick up where they'd left off in June. It was time to resume his life among the people who knew and cared about him in Alaska. It was time to get back to his life. He would rather eat rocks.

The summer on the farm had been the best season of his life. He and Ed had worked the land hard, and the land had worked them. Compared to summers on the boat, where the days were tedium stacked on tedium, farming was an outdoor action program. Norman had been out in the dirt and sun every day, plowing, hoeing, mending fences, burning brush, dragging irrigation pipes, fixing motors, pruning peach trees, and picking peppers, tomatoes, and cantaloupes. His hands were hard and dark. His body was strapped with new muscles, and his never-seen-the-light Alaska skin shone brown and vital.

"The girls back home won't stand a chance," Ed had teased on the way to the airport that morning.

"What girls?" Norman had quipped. Laura Magruder had faded in his heart like an old picture. He felt not just strong, not just tan, but free. The time with Ed and Emily's family had been a long vacation from his life. He could even laugh about it now, thanks to Ed's unique coaching over the summer.

"So let me get this straight—you called her and she hung up."

"Yes."

"And then you called her back and she hung up."

"Yeah."

"And then, let me guess, you called her back?"

"Mm-hmm."

"That is just plain pitiful, buckaroo. Pitiful."

They laughed, and that was the last time he'd called her. That had been his fifteenth birthday, and his independence day. Being around Ed Flannigan and being pitiful just wouldn't mix.

Ed treated him like he already knew the stuff he was supposed to learn. He wouldn't show Norman how to change the oil on the tractor and then tell him to do it. He'd just tell him to do it.

"Come get me if you have any trouble," he'd say, and walk away like it was all taken care of.

It was so easy not to mess things up for Ed. Nothing like how he felt around home. His parents didn't even seem to think he could find his way back.

"Do you have clean clothes to wear on the plane?" his mom had asked on the phone the night before.

"Yeah."

His dad chimed in on the other extension, "You've got your money in a safe place?"

"Yeah."

"You'll have a layover in Seattle for an hour or so," his dad informed him, as if he couldn't read his own stupid ticket. "Don't leave the airport."

"You can ride the trains and escalators for something to do," his mom offered helpfully. "We'll all go shopping for school clothes when you get to Anchorage."

"Great," Norman said obligingly, but the thought of a Tuttle family dork-o-rama school clothes shopping trip was all he could take.

"Listen, I gotta go," he lied. "Ed needs me to do one last thing in the shop. See you in Anchorage."

Norman had wandered out to the barn and pulled the chain on the single lightbulb. The rusted tractor rested just inside the door. Snatching a greasy rag from the workbench, he began the familiar routine. Pop the radiator cap and dip a finger. Okay. Pull the oil pan dipstick, wipe, replace, pull again. Just right. He gave the fan belt two solid tugs. Good.

"That old tractor won't know what to do without you," Ed said from the open door.

Norman recovered from the surprise, then pointed. "Keep an eye on this belt. It wants to come loose."

"We'll be fine." Ed came over and tugged the belt once. "How about you?"

"I'm fine."

"I heard you talkin' to your folks. How's all that goin'?"

"Same." Norman dismissed the question and all the people in it.

"Don't let it bug you, buckaroo." Ed took the rag from Norman's hand and used it to sweep the dust from the engine cowling. "It's just like you and this tractor have been all summer. You check this, you check that. Most of the time everything is okay, but you'd never know if you didn't check, would you?"

Norman didn't have to answer. He'd learned when Ed was asking questions and when he wasn't.

"That's what parents do with their kids." Ed tossed the rag back to Norman and pulled the light chain. "We check on them all the time. Just in case. It lets them know they belong to us."

"But I don't want to belong to anybody," Norman said as they ambled back across the yard.

"Oh, you do. Believe me about that one, Norm. You do."

The terminal, with the hustling crowds and announcements and stores and cafés, had a festival feel about it. Norman wished it belonged to him. Every face a stranger, and everything under the sun at his fingertips. Ed Flannigan had given him his final pay all in cash, and he felt the weight of five hundred dollars of it in his pocket as he reluctantly walked up to the counter for his connecting flight to Alaska.

"I'm sorry, but that flight has been canceled due to mechanical problems," the ticket agent informed him. "The next flight to Anchorage will be departing at seven p.m."

Norman looked at the clock on the wall. "That's six whole hours!"

"That is correct." The agent glanced up at the long line of

disgruntled passengers forming behind Norman. "Shall I confirm you on that flight?"

Norman nodded, handing the woman his ticket. He wondered if a guy could burn up six hours riding around on the shuttle train and escalators and blowing money at the gift shops. Like a horse left in the corral too long, Norman had forgotten what to do when the gate was finally left open. He failed to comprehend the open range at all until the woman handed him back his ticket.

"There are regular shuttle buses to downtown if you'd like to see some sights and do some shopping." She said it with such a confident face that Norman thought it sounded much like permission, if not an out-and-out order.

"Thank you," said Norman, suddenly flush with capability. "I might do that."

His parents would already have left for Anchorage, he told himself, so there was no point calling. They'd figure out his flight was late when they got to the airport. Norman followed the signs to the bus stop, bought his round-trip ticket for downtown, and stood in line with the other stranded passengers who sought distraction and distance from the airport.

Norman, for his part, had already decided what he sought: clothes. What kind, he didn't know. But real clothes. The thought of starting another school year in a mother-selected wardrobe gave him the willies. Those oddly checkered shirts from J. C. Penney, and three-for-one slacks from the back-to-school sale tables at roadside strip malls. Two sacks of three-pack Jockeys and a bale of socks. Topping it off would be the obligatory new blue nylon goose-down pillow coat.

"That'll keep you warm!" she'd say.

The overall fashion effect was that of an assistant camp counselor at a low-rent Bible retreat.

No more, Norman thought as he climbed aboard the bus in his tractor-stained, high-wader jeans and the dusty no-name sneakers on his feet. A young man doesn't spend the summer on the outskirts of a college town and not figure a few things out. He was fifteen years old and knew it was time to find his own way in the clothes department. He had no clear idea which way that was, but he knew which way it wasn't. If he didn't see what he liked in a place like Seattle, then it probably didn't exist. Norman knew it was time to move beyond cotton-wool layering, rubber, and goose feathers. It was time for some clothes that said *Norman.*

These were the thoughts that stirred in Norman as he gaped at the gradual buildup of the city scene on the way in from Sea-Tac Airport. Grunge might well have been founded on the beat of a young man's heart in a situation like this. To go where no Tuttle had gone before. To go where no Tuttle had even wanted to go before. His parents would have a whale when they found out. Maybe they'll send me back to Oregon to teach me another lesson. Ha!

When the bus nudged into the surface traffic between the tall buildings downtown, Norman nearly swooned. The amounts of vehicles, stores, restaurants, and people were in-comprehensible to a kid from a fishing family in Alaska whose biggest adventure in life to date was spending a sum-mer on a small farm near a small college in Oregon.

Norman Tuttle was aware that his life story would not be appearing on the Biography Channel anytime soon, but he felt things were definitely looking more interesting as he was taken into the heart of the city. He saw Musicland, Leather Land, hot tacos, and Cantonese cuisine—whatever that might be. It didn't matter to Norman. It just mattered that it was here, and it was not where he lived. There were five-story department stores, megaplex movie houses, and danc-ing-naked-lady places. There was more to a city block of Seattle than his entire town back home in its most preten-tious aspirations. Their stupid Winter Carnival wouldn't even be noticed on these overflowing streets.

Norman was drawn into the pedestrian flow before he had a chance to resist. The human current flowed down the side-walk carrying Norman with it. He brushed against buildings and parking meters. A street musician sang in his face one instant, a panhandler put an open hand to it the next. Barely aware of his legs moving, Norman let himself be swept along until he was finally deposited at the mouth of Pike Street's rambunctious open-air market and merchant fair.

Pausing only long enough to catch his breath, Norman plunged in. He made his way past the jokey fishmongers without temptation. He'd seen a lifetime of fish. He barely looked at the produce stands. A summer spent growing vegetables, peaches, cantaloupes, and watermelons will take the luster off a red pepper no matter how bright they polish it.

But when Norman finally squeezed past the edibles, the merchandise became more inviting. There was jewelry, and leather, and T-shirts with things written on them that Norman wasn't even allowed to say in the house. He sorted through some of these just for sport. Then his eye was captured by a large silver cross on a thick black cord. The styling suggested mystic kings, the Pope, and the Nazi officer corps all dangling from the same string. It was blasphemous, ostentatious, and expensive. His mother would not have bought this for him if it had been marked 90 percent off half off wholesale. His mother would never think of even picking such a thing up off the street. His mother would probably not let it in the house.

It was perfect.

The woman behind the table was an utter pincushion of jewelry. Every hole or fold of skin on her face had a piece of hardware bolted to it. Norman figured you could fix a tractor with what she had screwed to her ears alone. She wore finger-less black leather gloves with studs on the knuckles, and she had the complexion of a person who sleeps under her car.

"That's forty-five dollars," she said, looking Norman up and down as if doubting a person like him could have that kind of money.

Norman tugged at a couple of bills in his pocket, trying not to show the whole wad but anxious to prove his buying power. The money seemed to have taken root there, and when he snatched at the loosening bills, the ball of money exploded from his pants in a shower of cash. Twenty- and fifty-dollar bills scattered at Norman's feet.

Abandoning any shred of composure he had, Norman threw himself on the pavement, groping for the loose bills. A passerby, unaware of what was going on, scuffed a fifty with his foot and sent it skidding out of Norman's reach. Still on his knees, Norman hustled after it, but just as he was upon it, a black boot came down hard on the bill, pinning it to the concrete.

"That's mine!" Norman said to the boot.

A voice from overhead spoke calmly. "I saved it for you."

Norman looked up and met the eyes of a boy about his own age who smiled at Norman and shook his head. "Man, you really shouldn't be flashing your dough. There's bad people around this place." The boy lifted his foot and Norman recovered the money.

"Thanks." Norman stood and took a good look at this surprise ally. The boy had long straight black hair on one side of his head. The other side was dyed the same color orange as a life jacket. His leather coat had white paint splashed on it and a piece of steel cable draped around the collar. Must be a construction worker, Norman thought. His shirt was fishnet, which looked extremely breezy and uncomfortable to Norman, but maybe not altogether bad. His jeans looked to have been removed from the victim of a car accident, and his sturdy black boots stood resolutely beneath him.

Norman could see this was a style not likely to find its way home from the Tuttle family shopping spree in Anchorage. But as good as it looked, he wasn't sure about the kid inside the clothes. Extending a cautious hand, he repeated, "Thanks," and turned away to finish his transaction for the cross.

Stuffing the wad of bills back into his jeans, Norman noticed the other boy still standing to the side of him.

"Nice stuff," he said, approving Norman's purchase, then stuck out his hand in an unlikely position—like to shake hands, but not.

"My name's Tango," the boy finally said, putting his hand down after Norman neglected to take it.

Norman put the medallion around his neck. "I'm Norma . . . I'm Norm Tuttle."

"Keep cool, Norm Tuttle," Tango said, and vanished into the passing shoppers.

Norman continued working his way down the booths, looking for his next impulse, keeping his eye out for a leather jacket like Tango's, but maybe without the ironwork and paint. Or maybe a pair of those boots. A T-shirt with the words Dysfunctional Child etched across it was purchased with a grin and quickly pulled over his plain, dull work shirt. A wide leather belt with a silver buckle and a thirty-dollar price tag was soon hugging his waist. Looking better all the time, he thought.

At a booth of hand-carved wooden bowls and wall plaques, Norman spotted a familiar passage. *Surely goodness and love will follow me all the days of my life—23rd Psalm*. His mom would like that. As he paused to consider it for her, the aroma of pizza drifted by. His growling stomach reminded him that he hadn't eaten lunch yet, and he set out to find the source of the smell.

Sitting at the crowded counter with his slice, Norman was startled to look up and see Tango perched on the next stool. "Tango, hi!" he blurted out, tapping the boy on the shoulder.

Tango spun around and with a look of surprise said, "Hey, if it ain't Norm Titter."

"Tuttle," Norm corrected, feeling a little bit like a man of the town, having just been recognized by a local and all. "You live here?"

"Yeah. Seattle. Greatest city in the world," Tango said like a chamber of commerce rep. "You?"

"Alaska," Norman said almost apologetically.

"Alaska?" Tango slapped Norman on the shoulder. "I never met no Alaskan before. What you doing here?"

"Um, hangin' out, I guess." Norman took a bite of his pizza and groped for the coolest answer. "Trying to find some clothes, you know, like, stuff."

"Clothes?" Tango lit up. "What kind of clothes?"

"I dunno," he said honestly. "Maybe a jacket or something." He pointed at Tango's jacket with his crust. "Maybe something like that."

"Like this?" Tango looked flattered.

"Yeah, well, sorta like that."

"Well, you're talking some big bucks for something designer like this, Norm of Alaska."

"I've got money," Norman said proudly, unconsciously touching the roll of bills in his pocket. "But I don't have much time. Where can I find one around here?"

Tango narrowed his gaze at Norman, sizing him up. He appeared to think something over, then leaned in closer and lowered his voice. "I tell you what, Norm Tuttle. I like you, and I know a dude in the wholesale clothing business that likes me. I get all my stuff at half price."

"Half price?" Norman's first thought was that his parents would be proud of him, which was incredible considering that he would have to fight his father just to get these clothes in the house. "Can I get half price?"

Tango sat back again, sizing him up. Thinking it over. "Down from Alaska. On your own in the big city. You're my kind of man, Norm Tuttle. I think I can hook you up with something." Tango slid off his stool and walked out of the pizza place. "C'mon, Norm Tuttle. You'll be glad you ran into me."

Norman fell in cautiously behind Tango's jaunty gait, but it felt better with every step. Here he was in a city full of strangers and he already had a friend. At least a business connection. It felt good to lope down the sidewalk acting local with a local. Tango was a real city kid and Norman was soaking up the moves. They carved a path down the center of the sidewalk. Tango seemed to enjoy slamming shoulders with the people who passed the other way, answering their insults with those of his own. Not Norman's style, but he stayed silent and tried to keep up.

They turned onto an emptier street leading down to the waterfront. Norman was relieved to be away from the crowds. "What kind of name is Tango?"

"It's just what my friends call me," Tango answered. "What sort of name is Tuttle?"

Norman was unimpressed by the return question. "I dunno. Family name. English or something. I think it means 'boring.'" Norman sneered at his own joke, but Tango wasn't listening.

"Oh," he said absently, his eyes now fixed on a graying vagrant who was polishing a parking meter with a red rag. "Look at that crazy old man. These bums are making this city a bad place to live. Watch this."

As they walked by, Tango reached out and roughly snatched the man's hat, a well-worn leather driving cap, and took off.

"Hey, that's my good hat."

Norman heard the man calling behind them as he ran to keep up with his new friend, though he was no longer sure why. Tango darted into an alley, and Norman ducked in behind him. "Why'd you do that?"

Tango plopped the cap on Norman's head. "Why not? It's free, man. Throw it away if you don't like it."

Tango continued down the alley and Norman followed more slowly. Tango's mean spirit had caught Norman by surprise. He pulled the hat from his head and finally took stock of what he was doing.

He'd told a total stranger he had money and then followed him into a dim alley in a huge city Norman didn't know from

Mars. He flushed with the stupidity of it, and the hackles on his neck rose.

Suddenly, where just moments ago had been shadows and doorways, there was company. Three other boys the same basic age as Tango were standing around him in the alley with coyote grins. In the middle of them, with the toothiest grin of all, stood Tango. "I told you, Norm of Alaska, there's bad people around here."

Norman felt his new farmer muscles tighten in his shoulders. He balled his fists like he'd done only one other time in his life. "You can't do this," he said, trembling.

"Don't be pitiful, Norm Tuttle. Give it up." Tango walked straight toward him, arm raised, as two of his confederates closed in beside Norman.

"You can't do this!" Norman roared. His fists flew and his voice echoed down the brick alley.

"Tuttle, Tuttle, Tuttle. Tuttle comma Norman. Tuttle, Tuttle, Tuttle."

Norman woke to the sound of his name. A blurry silhouette of a man moved in front of him as his mind tried to make reality out of a fragmented scene. His face lay against the damp bricks, and his head pounded. When he moved, the silhouette stopped suddenly.

"What's this? A boy! Are you hurt?" The man squatted down and put his face right in Norman's.

Norman smelled the breath of a dog, but through his hazy vision and mangled judgment he saw the face of his father. "Dad—help me." The words sounded muffled and far away. His tongue felt like fried liver.

The shadowy man pulled Norman up by his shoulders and leaned him against the wall. He took off his coat, put it behind Norman's head, and spoke in a kind voice, like a child to a troubled pet.

"I'm not your dad, I'm a friend. My name is Oliver. Do you know who you are?"

Sitting upright, Norman felt his head begin to clear, and his sight returned enough to see the man from the street whom Tango had harassed. "My name is Norman. Norman Tuttle."

"Oh, what luck!" The man held up Norman's ticket envelope. "I just found these." The odd man spread the envelope to show Norman's plane ticket and the bus pass to the airport and pointed with a greasy finger. "See? Tuttle comma Norman. Tuttle, Tuttle, Tuttle. What a fine name. Too good to lose."

Oliver pressed the tickets into Norman's hand, then noticed something on the ground beside him. "My hat! Oh, this is a lucky day! I thought it was gone for good."

Norman's mind was waking further, now just slightly clouded with the aching throb. He patted his empty pocket, checked for the missing necklace and the belt, then slumped against the wall again. "You didn't lose your hat. It was stolen by the same guys who took my money—Tango and his gang of friends."

"Tango." Oliver nodded sadly. "I know that bunch. Bad eggs, every one of 'em. Come on, Norman Tuttle, get up off that damp ground."

Norman stood with the man's help. He seemed to be all right. His new shirt was torn across the front, and his face was tender. Rubbing a fist-sized knot on the back of his head, he winced. He probed a tender place around one eye and then noticed his scuffed and swollen knuckles. He'd gone down swinging, at least. He looked around the alley some more, hoping to see one of them in the same shape he was in.

"Wow. I got mugged!" Norman was impressed and partly pleased with the idea, already thinking of telling the story. He bet nobody back home had ever been mugged. The thought of home brought a sudden panic. "What time is it?"

The older man dug deep and methodically inside his layers of clothes, finally producing a cheap pocket watch with a cracked face. "It's nearly six o'clock."

"I have to get back to the airport! I'll miss my plane!"

Norman started one way down the alley, then stopped and went the other, then stopped altogether. "Where *is* my bus? Where am I?"

"This way, Norman Tuttle." The man steered Norman by one arm toward the light end of the alley. "I know that bus. I got on it once by mistake and spent a month at the airport. Didn't like it much. Too noisy to sleep."

Norman had never been in the company of a genuine homeless person before. "Do you really sleep on the streets?"

Oliver looked at him, astonished, as they turned up the hill toward the busy intersection. "Of course not! I sleep under them! It's much safer."

Norman took it as a joke and laughed. The man laughed too, just to be agreeable, and they continued in silence to the corner.

"Your bus should be leaving that hotel there in a few minutes. Can you make it alone?" He stood looking carefully at Norman, watching for any unsteadiness. "Do you know where you're going?"

"Yeah. Yeah, I'm all right. Thanks for your help, um, Mr. . . . ?"

"Oliver. Just plain Oliver." He shook Norman's hand and pointed him across the street. "You go on now. I've got more work to do, Norman Tuttle Tuttle Tuttle."

The man turned and walked down the street, making a

song out of Norman's name. "Tuttle tuttle tuttle now I know a boy named Norman Tuttle."

Norman reached the other side of the street and turned to see him moving slowly along, the rag in his hands again, wiping parking meters as he sang quietly to himself. Norman let out a heavy breath. Still dazed, he watched the bent man work his way down the sidewalk and blend with the press of shoppers.

Oliver, he thought, watching him go. His head cleared a little more as the shuttle bus pulled up in front of him. *Oliver?* Norman dashed around to the end of the bus to have another look, but the man was gone.

Norman climbed aboard, gave the driver his ticket, and sat in the first seat, still staring out after the man. No way, he thought, probing the five-hundred-dollar lump on the back of his head. There's just no way.

The bus grumbled away from the curb and nudged into traffic. Norman turned his back to the window, no longer interested in the city sights. His eyes tried to drift closed, but he forced them open again. He would not let his guard down in this place anymore. The driver stole appraising looks at Norman in his big mirror: the torn shirt—Functional Child—and the bruised face. The bloodied hands.

Finally he asked, "You all right, kid?"

"I will be," Norman said, knowing that was true.

"You know where you're going?"

"Alaska," Norman answered, flagging his airline ticket wearily.

The driver looked at him a while longer, as if deciding whether or not to believe it. "You belong to somebody up there?"

"Yeah," Norman said, realizing it at the same time he said it. "Yeah, I sure do."

AFTER THAT

Things got better. Norman cleaned up as best he could on the plane, but by the time he stepped into the terminal in Anchorage, he had a black eye that he couldn't have hidden behind two hats. He was eight hours later than his mom and dad had expected, and he spotted them sitting in the hard chairs across the way. A stuffed polar bear appeared to stalk them from behind. Franky, Jessie, and Caleb were rolled up in new coats on the floor, dead asleep.

His dad saw Norman first and poked his mom once in the arm. They both jumped to their feet, and Norman held up his hands the way someone might do to stop a bus. To Norman's surprise they stood still and waited. As they stood there, his mom looking scared, his dad just puzzled, Norman couldn't help it. He smiled. For the first time since he could remember, it was good to see his parents again. Really good.

"What in the world—" his mom started.

"Where have you been?" his dad interrupted.

His mom laid a cool hand alongside Norman's sore face. His dad looked mad, but Norman knew he wasn't, because he reached out a hand and held Norman's arm as if to steady him.

Norman looked him in the eye. "I messed up."

"I see that," he said.

"I got myself mugged. Wanna hear about it?"

Something about the way he said it brought the glimmer of a smile to his dad's face. "Wouldn't miss it."

Norman bent down and scooped up the sleeping Caleb while his mom roused Franky and Jessie. His littlest brother woke just enough to recognize who he was, then wrapped his little legs around Norman's waist and went back to sleep on his shoulder.

"Let's go home," Norman said to nobody in particular.

"Sounds good to me," his dad said, hoisting Jessie onto his back.

"What about your new school clothes?" asked his mom, brushing dirt from a sleepy Franky's new blue goose-down coat.

"If you don't mind, Mom," Norman said over his shoulder as he led the way out of the terminal, "I'd like to pick out my own clothes this year."

"Of course," she said, untroubled by the notion.

I guess it's as easy as that, Norman thought. Tell 'em what you're doing. Ask for what you want. He slowed up and fell into step with his dad.

"Hey, Dad?"

"Yeah, Norm?"

"You got any pictures of Uncle Oliver?"

"Somewhere, I'm sure. Why?"

"I'll tell you all about it on the way home," Norman said, boosting his baby brother higher on his shoulder and stepping through the automatic door into the fresh Alaska night.

TOM BODETT is a renowned writer and commentator and the first and only spokesperson for Motel 6, the national motel chain. He made his national broadcasting debut in 1984 as a commentator for National Public Radio and went on to host *The Loose Leaf Book Company*, a national radio program about children's literature. He also hosted the PBS/Travel Channel co-production *Travels on America's Historic Trails with Tom Bodett*. He has several books to his credit, including *Williwaw!*, his first novel for young readers.

Tom Bodett lives with his family in Vermont. They try to spend the long days of summer at their remote cabin on Kachemak Bay in Alaska.